THE BROKEN TRAIL

After a gang of robbers tries to kill him on the trail to Coker, Cody is lost and wounded. When he finally arrives in town, the corrupt sheriff blames him for the murder of a prominent citizen, who was slain by the same gang. Cody vows that he will unleash death and destruction on the men who embroiled him in this fight — but he has been thrown into a tiny cell, falsely identified by the widow of the dead man, and today, without trial, he must hang . . .

ALEXANDER FREW

THE BROKEN TRAIL

Complete and Unabridged

LINFORD
Leicester

First published in Great Britain in 2015 by
Robert Hale Limited
London

First Linford Edition
published 2017
by arrangement with
Robert Hale
an imprint of The Crowood Press
Wiltshire

A catalogue record for this book is available
from the British Library.

ISBN 978–1–4448–3163–4

Published by
F. A. Thorpe (Publishing)
Anstey, Leicestershire

Set by Words & Graphics Ltd.
Anstey, Leicestershire
Printed and bound in Great Britain by
T. J. International Ltd., Padstow, Cornwall

This book is printed on acid-free paper

1

He could hear the hoofbeats pound as the ones who had harmed him rode away on the Santa Fe trail. Cody could not see the riders because his eyes were closed and his mouth was full of dust. He was fast losing consciousness and he could feel the wetness of precious lifeblood dripping from the wound on his forehead. Then an awful blackness swallowed him and he thought of nothing else for an endless stretch of time.

When he half-awoke he opened his eyes painfully, keenly aware of a sharp pain in his head and the dull ache in his side. He was stretched out in his buckskin clothes and saw the dead colt lying just a few yards away; clearly its brains had been blasted out by a shot from a powerful weapon, possibly a shotgun.

He managed to half rise, feeling the ache in his forehead where the blood had already started to clot and turn crusty in the hot sun. The black flies rose in the air from where they had been feeding on it. If the wound were not attended soon infection would set in. But he would be dead long before that if he had to remain out here in the desert. He would not die from the heat, even though it had weakened his sinewy body as the time wore on; instead he would die from the freezing temperatures that prevailed in the desert once the sun went down. His body was young and hale, but even as he moved towards the dead animal he felt a terrible weakness pervade his frame and he almost fell again.

The dead horse was lying atop his bedroll and other supplies and his only chance of survival lay in getting the pack from under the supine animal. Then, at least, with water to drink and bedding to wrap in, he would have some chance of survival when the night came. Even in his befuddled state he knew that his chances of survival lay in what he was able to do in the next few minutes. If he could not get his supplies free the chances were that he would be dead within the next few hours.

He groaned again, this time at the pain in his side. The sound from his lips was thick, blurred, so parched were his mouth and throat.

Some of the coarse rope that lashed the pack to his saddle was visible. He gave this a tug, hurting his hands in the process, but the animal was literally a dead weight and nothing happened. What little fluid was left in his body made his neck sweat and he could feel fresh blood ooze through the crusted wound on his forehead. He pulled again and the roll shifted beneath the carcass. Mustering his strength, he pulled with all his force. The strain was so great he fell backward, the impetus pitching him on to the road — if you could call this rutted, rocky depression in the desert a road.

For a moment he lay there. Cody, his name was Cody, that was all he knew. He had to survive. The longer he lay here the less chance there was of achieving that goal. Once more he forced himself up, turning his gaze from the dark-blue sky as he did so, focusing with all his might on what had to be done. It occurred to him how good it would be just to give up. He could lie here; let nature take its course, then all his suffering would end. Just as swiftly his mind rejected the idea. He had been treated with evil intent. He was going to keep going and survive.

The sun was still blazing down but it was clearly growing later in the day because the red orb was high in the sky. He heard the pounding of more hoofs and rolled towards his dead horse to get out of the way, because the noise he heard was the rumbling of heavy wagon wheels rattling round and round as the horses galloped towards the town of Coker, their destination. How he knew this was a mystery. As he rolled over, a startled, pale-yellow scorpion, a big one with a red stinger, rushed out from his jacket. It was hard to say which of them was the most startled, although the way his head felt when he moved it could have stung him to death and he wouldn't have minded much.

He was still kneeling when the wagon came into sight, pulled by two large bays. The cart was one of the old-fashioned kind once used by settlers all over the western states, still in use now, with a canvas-covered body, and iron hoops on the wooden wheels to make them functional in the rough conditions, with two seats up front. A man and a woman occupied these. The man was thickset, dressed in a brown suit with a high collar. He wore a soft fawn hat, and on his feet he wore dark brogues made of soft, expensive leather. He had a broad, fleshy face, a curly moustache below his slightly bulbous nose.

The woman beside him was slimmer but with a thickening of the waist that indicated impending middle age. She was dressed in a long blue dress, with a blue jacket, clothes that hugged her body, but with a slight hint of fashion that showed they had cost some amount of money. Her expression was one of kindly concern. Even at this stage of her life and in his physical state Cody could tell that she had once been a beautiful woman. Even as the heavy wagon rumbled to a halt — showing that it was laden with goods of one kind or another — a younger, stunning version of the woman rode up from behind on a black gelding. Long brown hair with a hint of red in the curls spilled out from under her bonnet. She looked at the damaged man with a fierce intensity that did not bode well for him. At that second another horse drew up on which sat a young boy who could not have been more than ten years old. The family, for it was obvious that this was what they were, stared at the young man.

'What happened?' asked the middle-aged man.

Cody surprised himself as he croaked out the answer between cracked, dusty lips.

'I don't know,' he said.

★   ★   ★

A ride followed in a space at the back of the covered wagon. There wasn't much room, because the wagon was filled to the brim with the kind of goods that people needed in the small towns miles from Tucson. Sacks of oats vied with drums of molasses, bags of dried peas, spades, picks, and cases of the new-fangled canned food containing stews, sausages and other necessities for those who worked out in the unfriendly desert.

The interior was a lot cooler than the desert and they had put down a horse blanket for him. He managed to half-sit as they went along, looking out of the back of the wagon to where the girl rode along. There was a fierce look on her face as she saw him peer out. She suddenly spurred her mount forward and rode beside her mother and father.

'We'd better drop him off in town.'

'Where?'

'I don't know, but he looks like trouble. He wasn't in that state for nothing.'

'Easy on it, Mary,' said Donald Sutton, with a wry grin at the attitudes of the young. 'He looks as if he needs help.'

'Well, give him over to Sheriff Pye. Pye can get in the doctor to tend to him.'

'Mary.' Her mother made the name sound like an exclamation. 'Pye will do no such thing. He'll throw him in a cell, see if he recovers, then find something to charge him with.'

'What about his story that he doesn't remember anything? Does that seem likely?'

'Mary,' said Donald, 'when you get to our age you learn that the world isn't a cut-and-dried place. We'll patch him up and he can go on his way in a few days and there'll be no harm done.'

The girl made no reply, letting the carriage fall in front of her, resuming her scrutiny of the back of the wagon, but there was no sign of the man they had picked up now. There was good reason for this: Cody was unconscious again and lay on his blanket without knowing a thing.

Coker was on the road to Tucson. It was a prosperous little place, built because it was on the way to the main cattle market, which meant that the cattle barons could house their herds there for indeterminate periods of time while waiting to bring them to sale. The town was also a way station for those who had been caught with gold fever. These individuals were often ill prepared, travelling this far before needing to replenish their supplies from the town on their way.

The town supplied other needs too, having two churches, three saloons and a hotel and dancehall that doubled as a whorehouse. There was also a jail, which was often fully occupied at the weekend when some of the herders went a little too far in 'whooping it up', as Donald liked to say.

Main Street had a number of stores, including his own. This was labelled prominently with a sign that said: 'Sutton's Hardware Supplies', painted in bright red and lined in black. Donald looked at the sign with pride.

'Looks good, don't it? Most striking sign in town.'

'Yes, Pa,' said Billy, their youngest, rolling his eyes. 'We going to unload this?' It had been a long, hot day haggling for the goods they would eventually sell. They had driven into the alleyway beside the store. Both Donald and his wife, Elizabeth, were chary of letting the public see them bring in stock, as this could be a lawless place. It wasn't unknown for men to be held up in public just for having an item one of the passing drifters wanted for their own. They also had another reason for going in the side door: a few people were going about their business including Ben Wilson, one of the town drunks. He stared at them on their arrival.

First they had to unload the injured man. Conscious now, Cody was able to get himself out of the wagon with a little help from the fierce Mary, stumble up the narrow stairs and into one of the small rooms above the shop where they all lived. Mary housed him in Billy's room, assisting him to lie on the trestle bed, but the bristling chin, the smell of stale sweat, the state of his clothes and the livid wound on his forehead revolted her.

She boiled some water on the stove, got a cake of carbolic soap and a towel and went upstairs to tend to the unwanted visitor. As far as she was concerned he was just another bother at the end of a particularly bothersome day, but it was less work than unloading the wagon. Carefully she cleaned, stitched and bandaged the wound, having seen that it was quite deep, then brought him some hot lentil soup. He was conscious most of the time during the cleaning process, only flinching now and then while she sorted him out. She saw that he was much younger than she had thought, probably only in his early twenties. He was silent after he had eaten. No wonder he was dazed, she thought, with a wound like that, but a little resentment rose in her that he had said nothing for all her efforts. The Suttons were Scots-Irish and there was a bit of the old fire in her veins.

'You should be all right in a few days.' She rose to go, but, as she turned, she found a strong hand seizing her bare arm. She turned in sudden fear and anger, saw him stare at her with those deep-brown, liquid eyes.

'Thanks,' he said, the strength suddenly going from his hand. He let her go and fell back on the feather-stuffed pillows.

'How is the young man?' asked her

father as they finished unloading the wagon.

'He's fine, I think he'll be out of it for a wee while.'

'He must be a kinda outlaw,' sang out young Billy. 'I want to hear what he did.'

'Now, you leave him alone,' said Billy's mother, Elizabeth, a humorous, sensitive woman, who had supported her husband fully when he wanted to open the hardware store in this small town. 'He'll talk — or not — in his own good time.'

'I don't want to know,' flared up Mary. 'He'll be gone as soon as he's better. I'll see to that.' She did not know why her parents both smiled at this declaration.

★ ★ ★

Later that night, Mary, who now had to share a room with Billy — it was either that or sleep in the parlour because there wasn't a lot of space above the

13

shop — heard a noise coming from the next room. It wasn't loud, barely above the sound of mice scratching, but she was young, her hearing was acute, and she wasn't as exhausted by the events of the day as the rest of the family. She flung on a housecoat, sat up and waited until she heard the soft shuffle of feet on the wooden stairs, then opened her own door.

When her father had the store built he had made sure that it had a large window looking down from the wall at the stair landing so she was able to make out the shadowy shape of the tall young man as he moved softly downwards, holding on to the wooden rail and taking his time. She followed swiftly when he was nearly at the bottom of the stairs. She was just about to challenge him when he turned and seized her in his arms. She gave a muffled squeal and immediately he let her go.

'What the hell is going on?' she demanded.

They were now standing beside the main doorway of the shop. Some light filtered in from the main window from the street beyond.

'I've got to get out of here.'

'Why?'

'I have to get the ones who did this to me.'

'Who were they?'

'That's what I don't know; at the moment all I know is my name, Cody.' His voice sounded confused. She saw that he was swaying. Mary didn't want him here, but she was a fair woman and had Christian values.

'You're in no fit state to go anywhere,' she said.

'It's important I get to them. I just . . . I need to go.' He began to unbar the door.

That was when they heard the sound of thunderous knocking. Cody sprang away from the door and into the shadows at the back of the shop. He tried to open the side door but this, besides being bolted, was firmly locked against thieves.

'Open up in the name of the law!' thundered a voice she knew well, that of the sheriff, Samuel T. Pye.

'Go away,' said Mary, 'my family has no business with you.' By this time her father and mother had appeared at the top of the stairs with day clothes hastily flung atop their night attire. Billy peeked out from behind them, thoroughly enjoying himself.

'What's going on?' asked her father, coming down to her side.

'Open up, or by the authority vested in me as the sheriff of this town, I'll break down this door,' shouted Pye, who was not a subtle man at the best of times. Donald hastily complied with his wish. The sheriff stood in the doorway holding a gun in one hand and a lantern in the other. He was flanked on either side by town businessmen, both of whom Donald knew well — indeed had indulged in the odd drink with them. One was the owner of the town's biggest saloon, Jackson Taylor, while the other was Bud Clemens who owned a liquor store along the road. They both carried shotguns, and wore expressions that indicated they were prepared to use them. Sheriff Pye was a large man with a pronounced gut, reflecting the fact that he could eat and drink for free seven days a week. He had a big face too, which habitually wore a superior grin showing tombstone teeth. He wasn't a well-liked man, but he was powerful, always turned up when he was wanted, got the job done, and kept the town clean of rogues. Now he held up the lamp and peered into the store, the feeble light barely penetrating the dark shadows.

'Where is he? Upstairs?'

'This is my property, Sam, you've got to have a good reason for coming in.'

'We're looking for a wanted man. He's been doing some bad stuff out of town. You stay here, boys, I'll go in.'

Pye stepped forward into the building. The two men pulled back from the doorway. At that second in a coiled rush of energy fuelled by the possibility of being caught, Cody burst from the shadowy interior, past the startled lawman, between the two businessmen, and out into the street.

He might have got away with his bold move if it hadn't been for the fact that instead of trying to aim his shotgun, Clemens swung it by the barrel, thumping the young man between his shoulder blades. This sent a spasm of pain down his back and he sank to his knees in the dust. The sheriff sprang as much as his bulk allowed him over the boardwalk, levelling his gun at Cody's head.

'Move it and you're dead. Take him away, boys.'

Clemens and Taylor jerked the young man to his feet. Even then, despite the weakness caused by his wounds he struggled with them.

'Let him go,' yelled Mary, who stood on the boardwalk now, 'he hasn't done anything.'

Pye gave her a contemptuous glare.

'Missy, the Mosse gang were over at the homestead of a prominent citizen this day. There's a murder been done. We've got our man.'

2

'What's your name?' spat Pye as he faced the captured man.

'Cody,' said the young man, still straining against his captors, but held fast in their strong arms.

'Cody what?'

A confused look spread across the young man's face. 'I don't know.'

'Right.' Pye marched over to one of the corner cells. The jail wasn't much to look at, consisting as it did of an off-white, one-floored building in the middle of town, on Main Street. Inside, it held only three cells, with a big grey curtain on a rail in front of them that could be pushed across for what little privacy the prisoners were allowed. Each cell contained a wooden bunk, a blanket, a pail for obvious reasons, and very little else. Food and water could be handed in through the narrow space between the bars. Pye unlocked the door in front of him with a big iron key from the bunch tethered to his belt.

'OK, boys, throw him in.' The two men were burly; they complied with the request immediately showing great enthusiasm for their task. Cody had the wind knocked out of him as he slammed against one of the walls.

Before he could recover the cell door clanged shut. He stood up and pushed against the bars.

'What are you accusing me of?' he demanded hoarsely. 'Doesn't a man have a right to know?'

'You know what you've done,' retorted Pye. Clemens viciously butted the fingers of Cody's hands with the butt of his shotgun. The man gave a cry of pain and let go. Moving away from the door he sat tiredly on the bunk; his bandage, which had come loose during his arrest, fell unheeded to the ground. Now he sat in the semi-darkness, his features mostly hidden. Only his unfathomable eyes glittered at them from the depths of the enclosure, reflecting the dim light of the oil lamp. The vivid wound on his forehead was barely visible.

'You need to tell me,' he said.

'Shut it, dogweed,' said Pye. He nodded to his companions. 'You two come with me.'

Once outside he shook hands with the pair.

'Couldn't have done it without you, boys.'

'Reckon you've a liability there,' said Clemens.

'What do you mean by that, Bud?'

'He means that we should finish the job and say he tried to escape,' said Taylor, a deep hatred in his voice that could not be concealed. 'You know as well as I do that Jake was a boon to this here town. The amount of hard cash he brought to us local businesses, man was a legend.'

'I'll say,' put in Clemens. 'You know he came into The Golden Nugget and spent more in one afternoon than most cowpokes do in a month. I say we do this now and rid the town of a liability.'

By this time they were so close to Pye he could smell their liquor-filled breath. He held up his hands.

'Boys, this ain't a free-for-all. It's my job to uphold the law. We've got to get evidence against him. That's the way to proceed, else we've got the potential for a lot of trouble. If anything happens to a prisoner without proof it'll look mighty bad.'

'Then we'll do it,' said Taylor. 'Give him to us on the morrow, we'll ride him out of town and do the necessary.'

'No, there ain't proof yet. I'm the one who'll lose his job.'

'Tell you what, we'll take him out to the widder-woman,' said Taylor. 'She'll identify him all right, then we can do what's needed.'

''Sides, you benefited more than anybody,' said Clemens. 'Look at all the times Jake gave you a few dollars to turn a blind eye when his men partied a little too much and he wanted them back at the ranch.'

'I don't take bribes, Bud, if that's what you're implying. Look, I'll go see her myself — the widow, that is — an' we'll get this sorted out. Now get to bed; that boy ain't going anywhere.'

The three of them parted with a few hoarse cries of encouragement. Pye went to his home, which was so close to the jail he could have spat and hit it from his side window.

* * *

Lying in the corner of the adobe cell, Cody wrapped the rough blanket around his long, lean body. He was angry at what they had done to him, but he needed to sleep and get his strength back — if sleep would ever come, that was. He had the sharp hearing of a young man and the exchange outside the jail had been clear enough: he was being held responsible for killing this Jake. In their small-town minds his clear involvement with some

24

kind of violence made him stand out as a marked man.

His head hurt in two ways. He had an internal headache, along with the external throbbing of his forehead. Well, he could partly blame the girl for the second pain. The wound was already knitting together, which meant it caused more pain in the interim. At least someone had helped him. The Sutton family had showed him that there was some good in the world.

Armed with this thought he decided he was going to try and escape. He wasn't just going to go meekly to his death. He did not doubt if he was sent for trial in Tucson the case would be dismissed for lack of evidence. The problem was, the kind of people who ran a town like this had their own version of the law, one that didn't include a fair trial.

As he lay there engulfed in a weariness that was part physical and caused in part by the fog in his head, he thought his tired brain was hallucinating, because he could hear the voice of the girl.

'Cody, Cody, if that's your name, it's me, Mary.'

He looked around and noticed that the cell had a tiny, barred window. He forced himself to stand, despite the wave of dizziness that threatened to engulf him, so that his face was level with the bars. The girl was looking straight at him.

'How are you doing this?'

'I'm standing on the edge of a horse trough at the back of the jail,' she said briskly. 'Keep your voice down: the sheriff lives next door. He's canny, that one, he'll jail me too if I help you.'

'What do you want?'

'Why did they arrest you?'

'I suspect that town drunk you mentioned saw you helping me into your . . . house, and told the sheriff . . . ' He swayed.

'But why did they arrest a sick man?'

'They didn't know that,' he said,

managing a smile. 'They think I'm some kind of desperado.'

'It doesn't matter, they must have a reason for locking you up.'

'I'm some kind of suspect, it seems.' He went off on an apparently random tack. 'So do you know some kind of businessman called Jake who put a lot of money into this town?'

'Well, there's Jake Thatcher, he's known for investing in anything that takes his fancy. He has the Slash T just outside town.'

'So that's what they were talking about,' said the young man almost to himself.

'We have to get you out of here,' said the girl, 'otherwise you won't have a chance. That so-called lawman, he just bows down to business.' She turned her head. 'A light's come on,' she whispered. 'I have to go. Why did you ask me about Jake? Is he dead?'

'I haven't been accused of anything, but it seems I will be,' he replied.

'Goodbye,' said the girl, 'I'll do my

best.' Then she was gone.

Cody returned to his bunk. His body was young, but still recovering from the ordeal in the desert. Yet, despite the pain in his head and the dull ache in his side, allied with thoughts of Mary echoing around his head, at some point he closed his eyes and drifted off to sleep.

*   *   *

Jean made her way across the space in front of the ranch she had restored and built up with her husband. She was a tall, good-looking woman who at this moment wore dark garments befitting someone who had just lost her husband. Three years it had taken them to bring the property to this point, and in the past she had taken pride in the fact that they had purchased a ramshackle place from old Reynolds, converting it to a modern, efficient ranch in that time.

The Slash T now employed a goodly

number of men, besides owning a stockyard in town where cattle from other ranches were housed on their way to market.

Although she was a little past her prime, her full features and the blonde hair hanging past her shoulders assured that most men would give her a second glance. But for now she walked with the slow gait of an older woman, her spirit broken by the brutality of the events that had so lately happened. Her ears were caught by the sound of a horse trotting into the space. She turned and saw Pye was already dismounting. He tied his horse to a fence and strode over.

'Jean, how are you?' They were old — well, not exactly friends, but they had known each other for years.

'What's the news of the men who did this?' she asked grimly.

'Look, we ain't got the manpower to search a county,' said the sheriff, 'they'll be well away by now. The good news — if there is any — is that we think we've got one of the bastards.'

'Won't bring Jake back,' said Jean, her voice breaking a little.

'You still haven't told me why those roughnecks saw you as a target,' said Pye.

'I don't know. One of those things. They probably think we kept a lot of money on the premises.'

'You don't seem interested in the feller we've got.'

'I doubt if it's one of them. They seemed to know what they were doing.'

'Well, ma'am, your case is still a puzzle to me, but if you could come into town and identify this hound dog, at least we'll know either way.'

'How could it be?'

'Easy enough, this one's got a few injuries sustained in a rough and tumble. Looks to me as if they fell out with each other and turned on one of their own — happens more often than you might think.'

'Sheriff, my husband's lying dead in our front parlour in a storage box while

I'm waiting for old Dixon the undertaker. Do you really think I need this as well, on top of the rest?'

The sheriff regarded her with his black, glittering eyes. This, and his prominent hooked nose, combined with his dark clothes made him look like an old crow.

'Yes, I think you do.'

'All right, I'll do it, but it will be a waste of time.'

* * *

When Cody awoke he did not know where he was for a few seconds, then he swung his legs over the side of the bunk. It was barely eight in the morning. He knew this because the sheriff had put a big brassbound clock on the opposite wall above his desk. The clock was barely visible because the jailhouse was a shadowy place, very little light coming through the shuttered window at the front of the building. The small size of window and the shuttering were there for a reason: it was not unknown for a building like this to have a minor siege by those displeased that their companions had been taken into custody.

* ★ ★ ★

Assuming it was accurate, the young man had been out of the count for more than nine hours. After using the primitive facilities, Cody found that he had been left a jug of water and some dry bread and even a lump of cheese. It wasn't much, but good enough when you were hungry.

The anger that lay in him from the previous night stirred again. The steady throb in his head meant that he still could not marshal all his thoughts. He felt that he was always on the verge of knowing who he was and what had happened to him before the hard information was taken from him by the ghostly shadows in his mind. He wanted to beat at his own forehead in frustration as if this would unlock the secrets within, but given the fragile state of his wound it would have been an unwise move.

He was young; his body had enjoyed a reasonable sleep. This meant that he felt more like himself again — whoever *he* was. His returning strength was tested when he heard a noise at the barred window. He sprang back ready to take evasive action from a vengeful gun, when he saw it was the girl.

'You seem better,' she said. She was hatless and the morning sun high-lighted the redness in her hair.

'Why are you here?'

'Pa's opening the store. I just came to see if you were awake.'

'I'm OK.'

'Do you remember what happened at the Thatcher spread yet?'

'No, because I was never there. At least that's what I think.'

'Did you shoot him?'

'I don't think so, Mary, believe it or not. I don't feel like a murderer. I don't remember a thing before I got this wound, yet somethin' tells me it had nothin' to do with me. None of it makes sense — yet.'

'Don't say this stuff to the sheriff.'

'Why?'

'Just tell him, and anybody else, you weren't there. Otherwise he'll just blame you for the whole thing. Trust me.' She cocked an attentive ear. 'He went away first thing this morning, I don't know why, but that could be him coming back. I was up when he went — couldn't sleep for some reason. I've got to go.'

'Mary.'

'Yes?'

'Thanks,' said Cody. The girl flashed him a smile that made her pretty face light up, before slipping off her perch and vanishing into town. Somehow he knew she would be watching out for him from afar, as much as her duties for the day would allow.

The jailhouse door slammed open, framing the big shape of the sheriff and his two impromptu deputies. The sheriff stamped into the room, evidently not in the best of moods. His deputies parted and Jean, who wore a dark dress with ruffles of white lace, followed him. She walked in a desultory fashion, evidently uncaring whether she was there or not.

Light streamed in through the door, throwing the rest of the building into shadow.

'He's down here, Jean,' said Pye, leading her to the corner cell where the young man was housed. The light did not properly reach this part of the building, and her eyes had not had time to adjust from outdoor conditions.

Pye took out the hog leg from the holster at his side, and pointed it at the prisoner, who had retreated to his bunk so that he could be seen as nothing more than a vague outline.

'You,' he snarled, 'stand up and face the lady. I won't ask twice.'

Cody seemed of a mind not to obey, but then this was a load of nonsense anyway. His mind was disturbed, but he was certain that he had done no wrong. He stood up, moving towards the bars.

Jean took in his tall outline, his bristling chin, his too-long, tousled hair, and his profile as he turned away in resentment at being subject to such scrutiny. She gave a sudden scream, buckled at the knees and would have fallen, but for the help of the two merchants on either side of her.

'It's him,' she said, in a voice that was a combination between a gasp and a scream. 'He's the man who killed Jake.' Still half-collapsing she took a lace handkerchief from her sleeve as she tried to stem the tears that flooded from her eyes as the two merchants led her outside and into the carriage.

'She's lying,' was all the incredulous Cody could say.

'Shuddit, scum,' said Pye, his eyes boring into the shadowy prisoner. 'I'll deal with you in a minute.' He went out to where Jean sat in her carriage and pair with her driver. 'You're certain it's him? Do you want to go back in?'

'No. He is the man.'

'OK, that's good enough for me. You get out of here, you've had enough for the day.' She gave a grateful nod; her driver roused the horses, trotting them away in good order.

'Looks like you're murderin' scum after all,' he said to Cody, as he marched back into the jail.

'I didn't do anything.'

'I'll tell you what happened,' said Pye, fixing him with glittering black eyes. 'You Mosse boys wanted something from Jake Thatcher. You got it, and then killed him for your own reasons. Whatever you took caused you to quarrel when you were back on the trail. There was a fight; you were injured, Kane, then your murderin' brethren took off to go to their next robbery.'

'I'm not Kane, my name is Cody. Take me to trial. I'll show I'm innocent when I've had time to get my memory back.'

'What's that noise outside?' Pye walked out into the street to find a group of nine or ten angry citizens standing there. He recognized a couple of cattlemen, store men, the owner of the other saloon, Ty Landers. Jackson and Clemens joined them.

'You got to do somethin' now,' said Jackson. 'We got some mighty angry folks on our hands.'

'Know what? Now the critter's been identified I guess I ought to file the proper papers, manacle him and get him over to the court in Tucson. You folks is up for a little eye for an eye, but I can't be seen sanctioning what you want to do to him.' He slipped off the step and untied his horse from the hitching post and began to walk it along the road. 'Clem, walk with me.'

The angry men were going to follow the sheriff, but Jackson knew him well enough to hold them back.

'Looks like the prisoner escaped when I was out on other business,' said Pye, slipping a key to Clemens. 'By the

38

time I get to Four Trail Pass, for instance, the deed might well be done. Just impress these people to get out of the way.' He mounted his horse and rode off into town.

The knot of men was soon dispersed with the promise of a free drink from Jackson in his saloon. The men grumbled, but finally left. Then Clemens went inside, unlocked the door of the corner cell while Taylor pointed a gun directly at the prisoner's heart. When Cody came forward Clemens quickly went behind him, tying his wrists together with a length of coarse rope he had obtained from his own saddle-bag.

'Where's your sheriff friend, and where are you taking me?' asked the young man.

'To where justice will be done,' sneered Taylor. 'Now get out.' He jabbed the barrel of his gun against the prisoner's back and Cody stumbled out into the sunshine, blinking rapidly after the darkness of the cell. In his dazed mind it seemed to him that he was being taken away for trial. It was only after he was thrown roughly on to a buckboard being driven by Taylor, that he realized they were being driven in the opposite direction from Tucson. In fact he passed the very store in which he had been sheltering when captured, seeing it as he rolled around trying to escape.

As the buckboard left town the sheriff rode out and joined them, but only when he was not being observed. He was no fool, knowing that what they were about to do could lose him his job. The horse's hoofs thundered against the ground, drowning out any words any of them might have to say.

3

When they arrived at the place called Four Trails, one of which appropriately enough led to the widow's ranch, Taylor halted his carriage. On one side of them was a bluff that sheltered the area from the worst extremes of the desert winds so that there was concealment in the trees, bushes and grass growing at the side of the road. Just before the place where the trails divided was a large red rock of some vitreous material on one side and a clump of cottonwood trees on the other. Taylor purposefully halted beside these while the other two rode up and halted behind him.

Although Four Trails was not far from town it was so isolated it might as well have been on the far side of Mars. Cody was completely silent. He was a young man who tended to brood anyway and this was exacerbated by the hurts done to him over the last couple of days. He was in a deadly situation; he was wise enough to remain silent, alert, and optimistic enough to think there might be a way out of this almighty fix.

He had eaten a breakfast of sorts, consisting of the stale bread and cheese left by the sheriff, yet manna to his growling stomach, just before Jean's visit. He had also drunk copious amounts of water. This combined with the fresh air on the way out here had made him feel more like his old self again — whoever that was.

Cody knew that if he failed to prevail this stretch of road would be the last thing he would see. He had to pretend that he was still groggy.

'Right, boys,' said Pye, 'I have to remind you that what you're about to do is strictly illegal.' Clemens was already unrolling a thick length of rope he kept in his saddle-bag. He tied a loop in it, threw it over a high branch, brought it down, fed the end through the loop and pulled it through again. The rope dangled from the branch, so he tied a noose in the loose end. The casualness with which he did this chilled the blood of the young man looking on.

'You ain't no angel,' said Jackson, who was looking on from his big black stallion, Satan. 'What about the way you never questioned where Jake got his money from?'

'He was a mighty prosperous rancher. 'Course he had money.'

'Yeah, but we all heard rumours that when he came to Coker he brought all his transactions to the bank in gold,' said Clemens, 'unless he was a miner — and he sure wasn't one of them dirt busters. It's mighty suspect where that gold came from originally.'

'Tell you what,' said Taylor, 'this feller might know where the gold came from. I think the raid on Jake's place had somethin' to do with how he got his riches.'

'I don't know anything,' said Cody

from the buckboard, 'you're making a big mistake.'

He was blazingly angry with them, understandable in the circumstances, but did not want to show this was the case either by words or bearing.

'We could try beatin' it out of him,' said Clemens thoughtfully, spitting on the ground.

'Don't matter,' said Pye, 'get this over with before someone comes down here. 'Sides, there's a widow up there who's going to need comforting and who still has plenty of dollars in the bank. I lost my wife a while ago; you two are married and you ain't Mormons.'

'No, mine would cut my ears off if I went for another woman,' admitted Taylor.

'Or she would cut off something else,' said Clemens. 'Same goes for me. You dog, Pye, man's not even in his grave and you're talking about wooing his woman.'

'Mind you, he always had an eye for her. You could see it every time she encountered him in town.'

'Just get on with it.' Pye watched without emotion as the two men pulled Cody by the legs off the wooden boards of the carriage and on to the ground. Unable to check his fall as his hands were tied behind his back, he hit the ground with a jarring thud that took all the breath out of his body and made him writhe in agony. He did little to resist as the two merchants dragged him to his feet.

There was no more banter now as they grimly prepared him for his final moments. At first they tried to push him on to the back of the big black stallion without untying him but even their combined strength was not enough to do the deed. So Clemens untied him while Taylor levelled his .44 at the young man's chest.

Cody rubbed at his chafed wrists while cursing under his breath.

'Get up,' said Taylor, jerking his gun upwards.

Once the young man was mounted,

still firmly held by Clemens, the short length of hemp was tied around his wrists.

'You're hanging an innocent man,' said Cody. 'I've got nothing to do with this Mosse gang you're talking about.'

'You'll be telling us you've never heard of Mosse next,' sneered Clemens.

For one wild moment Cody considered hitting Clemens with a bunched fist, grabbing the reins and making a determined attempt to get away. For one thing was sure, the beast below him was capable of a great burst of speed. Unsure of who he was, or where he had come from, Cody was evidently a good judge of horses. A pity this rediscovery was coming at the moment of his untimely demise.

He stemmed the impulse as Pye, seated on his own mount directly in front of Cody, was the deciding factor. Even if he managed to swat Clemens away and snatch the reins, he would have to turn his horse round and gallop down one of the four trails before Jackson could fire. Conversely, he could not spring at the sheriff, who would leave his brains spattered across the road. Instead, by talking to the man, Cody was able to distract him while his hands were being bound. Another factor intervened when Clemens paused, and cocked his head to one side during the tying process.

'You fellers hear anything?'

'Yeah,' said Taylor, 'you shootin' off your big fat mouth. Get on with it.'

'Swear I could hear a noise in that high scrub over there.'

'Probably a bobcat. Get on with it.'

Cody played the old trick of pulling his shoulders forward while at the same time tensing the muscles in his forearms. Normally this would not have worked, but Clemens was in a hurry while at the same time distracted by whatever was in the bushes. He completed his task by putting the noose around the young man's neck while the sheriff looked on with an undue degree of satisfaction. As soon as the older man stepped back Cody relaxed his arms, straightened up in the saddle and began working on the ropes.

Pye trotted his horse out of the stallion's way now that the noose was in place. For Cody, time stood still although what happened next must have taken only a few seconds in real time. Just as Taylor raised his pistol to shoot his bullet into the air near Cody's horse in order to startle it into running forward, a shot came from the bushes and winged the shootist in the leg. Because it was fired from a distance it sounded like no more than the hum of a hornet as it winged the man. Taylor gave a muffled curse and fell to the dusty ground, clutching at the fleshy part of his thigh.

The stallion flared his nostrils and moved forward slightly, startled by this new development. Pye and Clemens turned their attention to the scrubland, both drawing their weapons and ignoring the cries of the wounded man in their midst.

Cody did not waste his chance. By using brute force he managed to free one of his hands from the hastily tied bonds. Urgently he pulled at the rope beneath his chin, knowing that he could still hang: more shots were being aimed at the scrub, and his horse was starting to whinny and trample at the ground.

Taylor, who was lying down groaning and clutching at his wounded leg, was nearly stamped on by the flailing hoofs and had to roll out of the way, begriming his clothes, hurting himself in the process on the stony trail.

Burning his hands on the hemp rope, Cody managed to get it free from around his throat. He would have marks on both his neck and hands but neither of those things mattered given that he was no longer going to choke to death. He still had the other rope tied around his right wrist where he had freed himself. Instead of proving a liability this turned into a boon.

Pye turned his attention away from

the bushes, saw the stallion dancing on the ground, dashed his horse across to the clump of trees and immediately lifted his pistol. Cody grabbed the reins of his horse and held them with one hand while he flailed out with the other, the loose part of the rope hanging from it like a whip. It hit Pye full in the face — they were that close — and he gave a scream of pain and fired his weapon wildly in the air, the shot missing by feet. Somehow, even though it hurt like hell, Cody managed to bring the big horse under control. He recognized in the animal a kindred spirit. It had been wasted on the man who was currently lying on the ground still screaming in pain.

At that moment Cody could have ridden away without being caught, perhaps with the added bonus of trampling over Taylor before his departure. On a mount like this he could be halfway to Yuma before sunset. He could probably find a lean-to on the way and rest there for the night. He could be out of the territory in two days.

He took a quick look around and saw that Pye was still rubbing his eyes where he had been stung by the coarse rope so there was no immediate danger from that quarter. The sheriff was also cursing profusely. Clemens, who was creeping towards the scrub, with his horse between his body and the bushes, caught Cody's attention. Suddenly he looked startled, ran forward with an almighty roar that seemed too loud for his wiry frame, and pounced on the mysterious attacker. Cody heard a scuffle.

He could have fled purely for self-preservation, but he dismounted and dived after Clemens. He seized the man by the shoulders and pulled him away from the figure on the ground. Clemens spun around trying to level his weapon at the young man, but Cody smashed him on the jaw, chopping down on his wrist at the same time. Clemens dropped his gun but swung wildly, connecting with the side of Cody's head. The blow made him dizzy, yet he swung a punch that connected with his rival's jaw again, with the sound of an audible click. Clemens fell to one side.

Cody turned his attention to the figure in dark clothes on the ground, hauling it upright. That was when a look of astonishment spread over his tense features. He was looking square in the face of his one prison visitor — Mary.

4

Mary!

Cursing to himself at the involvement of the girl, Cody took stock of what had happened in a bare second. She was wearing the riding clothes she had been dressed in when her family had rescued him from his fate in the desert the day before. Her green jacket was unbuttoned and she wore black trousers. In her hands she still clutched the lightweight rifle she had used to put paid to the hanging. She raised this instinctively when the young man loomed over her then let it fall by her side. Yet somehow, with long hair framing her soft face, she looked more feminine than ever.

'Come with me.' Despite the aches and pains in his body Cody bent over, and without hesitation pulled the girl up, managing with her co-operation to get them both into the saddle. He knew that he had knocked one man out, and the other was still rolling about on the ground, cursing the slug that had penetrated his calf. But there was still the sheriff, who would recover quickly from his temporary blindness to do some terrible damage. Pye would not like it to get out that he had aided and abetted in a hanging. The fact that there was a witness would mean that he could end up losing his career, such as it was in a small town like Coker. The important factor was that the inhabitants of the area did not like failure even if they didn't care about the odd hanging.

'Dabs is over there,' said Mary, indicating some large rocks to their left.

Cody did not waste any time, he urged the stallion forward in the direction she had indicated. Within seconds they were beside Dabs, a big mare that was quite happily chewing what little grass she could find on the scrub. The lush meadows in the Slash T were well out of reach on this dusty confluence of roads.

'I was keeping a lookout for what was happening in town,' said Mary, as she transferred from the stallion to her own horse. 'I saw the men going towards the jail and I ran to get Dabs. This isn't the first time this kind of thing has happened.'

'Where did you get the rifle?'

'It belongs to Daddy.'

The sound of a shot whistled through the air, showing that they were far from being out of danger. The sheriff did not appear through the rocks, the reason being quite obvious: Pye did not know what other weapons Mary might have to oppose him. For all he knew, Cody could be armed by now. Another two shots came their way at random. By that time, though, the two were already riding away.

'Are you going to hide in the hills?' asked the girl.

'No, I'm going back into town,' said Cody.

'Why would you do that?'

'There's a quote from somewhere about bearding the lion in his den,' said the young man shortly.

He seemed to have an unerring sense of direction, riding so well that he was able to take the lead. The girl followed without thinking too much about where he was taking her, admiring instead the horsemanship being displayed by the man whom she had so lately been taking care of, so it was with a startled air that she saw him stop before her father's hardware store. It was clear that the pair of them had arrived in town well before the sheriff. The reason for this was simple enough. Pye would have to look after his two companions, who were powerful men in Coker Town, making sure that they were able to get back safely.

Mary looked at Cody as he dismounted.

'What are you doing?'

'No use trying to hide from this bunch,' he said. 'Your family have already offered me hospitality, reckon I can impose on them for a little while longer.' He did not need to knock, the doors of the hardware store were wide open, and even as Mary reluctantly joined him Donald strode out, joined by his wife. Behind them came little Billy, who wore his shop clothes, as this was not a school day. He was having a ball, what with all this excitement going on. Coker Town was not a hub of action at the best of times. Donald was furious, but not with the young man. He snatched the rifle off Mary while Elizabeth grabbed her by the arm. Donald put down the weapon and grabbed his daughter off his wife.

'What the heck do y'think you're up to?'

'Don't be too hard on her, sir, she saved my life,' said Cody ruefully.

'That trio of evil men,' burst out Elizabeth, Mary's mother.

'Tell them, I have to help you,' said Mary. 'I'm going to lead you out into the hills, I know a shack where you can

57

shelter. Daddy, you can give him food and tools — '

'Mary, thank you for what you did, I probably wouldn't be here except for you.'

'Probably? I rescued you plain and simple, mister.'

'Well, that's what you say, but I'd already put a plan into action. Look, I'm grateful to you, but I have to get out of here.'

Mary struggled against her father, and vented a few choice curses that showed she had been hanging around a few cowboys in her short existence on Earth. Donald however, did not let her go.

'I'm not above paddling you,' he said.

'I helped him,' said the girl, 'and this is how he repays me. I hate you,' she said, glaring at Cody. He was already mounted on the black stallion. It was clear that he was not going to wait.

'You did me a great service,' he said, 'please leave it there. I'm grateful, ma'am.'

'I hope they shoot your stupid head off your shoulders,' spat the girl.

Elizabeth had gone into the store on seeing Cody get back on Satan. She came back with a burlap sack bulging with items of various kinds.

'Take this, and thanks for bringing back our girl.'

Cody took the bag. He gave a grateful nod to the couple and a smile to the girl then rode off in a flurry of dust.

'Billy,' said his father, 'stable that mare. This girl of ours can't be trusted with her.' He led the struggling girl inside. Mary freed herself at last.

'It's all right,' she said with the terrible dignity of the young. 'I've saved a life today, that will do for me. I hate him, though.'

She thought she saw a fleeting smile on both her parents' faces, but that surely couldn't have been the case.

★　★　★

Cody rode the big black horse towards the Slash T. The bitter gall of his situation bit into his soul. His dead horse had been a good steed as far as he could remember, but this big avenger was a horse made for his not inconsiderable skills. It made him wince with annoyance that he was going to have to let go of this superb steed in the not-too-distant future. Horse-thieving and trading was an offence in these parts where a good animal could make all the difference between poverty and prosperity. Satan, in turn, responded to the touch of someone who knew what he was doing, letting the speed rip from his hoofs, his long black flowing mane the only means Cody had of controlling him. It was as if his new master was giving him permission to let go with all his abilities and he was responding in kind. It would not be long, at this speed, before they were at the ranch.

Cody fulminated in his own mind over what had happened to him. He had been done a terrible injustice. If it hadn't been for his own efforts and a little help from the girl — all right, a *lot* of help — by this time he would have been swinging from the branches of a tree, one more victim of a lynch-mob system that suited a small-town mentality intent on finding scapegoats. He would have bet his last dollar, if he was fortunate enough to have any money, that he was just one in a long line of unfortunates who had been blamed for the troubles of Coker Town when really most of the problem was the place itself and how it treated its citizens.

Soon he came to the place where he would have been hanged. A rickety signpost indicated where the ranch was along with a couple of other destinations. He rode along the trail towards the Slash T but with a lot more caution than before, slowing Satan almost to a walk so that they slipped past the lush green meadows that were used to fatten the cattle before coming to a line of mesquite and cottonwood trees that concealed the building itself from view.

Cody knew then that it was time for him to walk rather than ride. That way he would be able to shelter and hide from any observers, yet still gain access to the building. The problem was, what to do with his horse? The young man did not have a piece of rope with which to secure him so he would have to rely on the animal remaining in the locality. Then he remembered the burlap bag that he had managed to keep in place at the back of the horse's neck as they rode. He rummaged in this and found that Elizabeth had included a length of rope.

Cody dismounted, and then tied the rope around the neck of the horse, speaking to him softly in a low voice and patting him reassuringly as he did so. Fortunately the big animal seemed to be quite tractable and allowed his new master to do what he wanted now that some of the fire had been taken from his hoofs. Also, the grass from the spring rains extended right to this area. Satan was already cropping some of the rich green fodder as Cody gave him one last reassuring pat and left him where he was.

Also in the bag was an old Remington Army six-shot percussion revolver quite often used by shopkeepers in places like Coker Town where someone might want to rob them of their dry goods or hardware. It seemed Cody knew a little about guns. He cursed softly to himself. It had few spare bullets. He supposed it would be of some use in a shootout and it was better than no protection at all.

He found a sheltered spot behind some more bushes that looked on to the area of the ranch itself. A long, low building, it was made from a mixture of traditional brick and adobe having a flat roof with clay pipes built in to drain off excess water. When it rained here it poured. Even as he watched, the widow herself came out of the building alongside a big, stolid-looking man with an unshaven chin who wore workday clothes consisting of dusty blue jeans, tan boots, and a dark shirt, stained under the arms. It was obvious that there was a master-servant relationship between them just from their body language, which was confirmed when Cody heard their voices, faint but clear enough even at this distance.

'Well, Mack, we're going to bury Mr Thatcher tomorrow. Most of the town will be at the funeral.'

'Yes, boss.'

'I suppose I am your new boss now, It will take some getting used to, Mr Stein.'

'Call me Mack. The men are mighty sorry about his killin'; he was a good man an' a good boss. At least you helped nail the bastard who did it.'

'You'll look after the business side of the place for me? The servants will take care of the house.' She ignored the comment about her part in identifying the killer.

'Surely, ma'am.' Mr Stein, it seemed, was a man of few words. He tipped his wide-brimmed hat to her, unhitched his horse and rode off. The widow turned and walked slowly back into the building, clutching a lace handkerchief, her long skirts almost rustling against the ground, the very picture of a respectable woman who had been robbed of her husband.

Cody felt the pain in his forehead and winced. It was because of this 'respectable' woman that he had nearly been hanged. Because of her he had nearly lost everything. Inside himself the voice of caution was telling him to get out of here before he was discovered and thrown to the dogs. If she really thought he had killed her husband, Jake, she wasn't going to show him any mercy. The fog inside his head was what decided his course of action. He still didn't have a clue as to who he really was and what he was doing in this area in the first place. No point in backing out now.

Quickly he assessed the situation. Stables and a bunkhouse flanked the adobe ranch. It was quite clear that both were empty, which meant that even at this time of day the men were out rounding up the cattle. Except for her personal attendants that meant the widow was in the building alone with her grief. Cody made his way along the side of the bushes, coming out at the very front of the ranch. He saw at a glance that the door was barred. Jean was taking no chances after what had happened a couple of days ago.

He went, instead, to the back of the building and found a window to what was evidently a kitchen area. These kitchens could be very stuffy in the heat of day, and someone had opened the casement. He listened for a while to make sure there was no one about then climbed in through the window, holding his weapon carefully so it would not go off. These ranch buildings had a pretty standard construction and he headed for the living area by pure instinct alone, his feet barely making a sound as they whispered over the earthen floor. This was going to be a lot quicker and easier than he thought.

Then before him he saw the new oak coffin lying in the centre of the front room on two thick trestles. He scanned the doorway quickly then stepped inside to beard the widow in her own space.

Until, that is, he felt the cold metal of a gun barrel at the base of his skull and heard the click of the weapon being primed.

'Who are you?' asked a cold, feminine voice. 'Give me a reason why I shouldn't kill you right now.'

$\star$ $\star$ $\star$

Back at his saloon, Taylor lay on the iron-frame bed in his luxurious bedroom with red and gold patterned drapes at the windows and thick red carpeting on the floor. He had a painting of the cavalry chasing Indians on the wall above his bed. At this precise moment he was resting on linen sheets in his shirt and long johns. The left leg was bandaged. The saloon owner had suffered the indignity of being brought back into town on the buckboard driven by his friend Clemens, the wheels rattling on the rough ground making him groan with pain at every turn, beside the humiliation of having to be helped inside his own saloon.

He was not in pain any more since Doc Gordon had given him some of that newfangled morphine to dull his senses. The doctor hadn't asked too many questions.

'That's a good clean wound,' he said, 'superficial wound in the fleshy part of the leg. You've had some loss of blood, but you should be up and about in a couple of hours.'

Taylor had not been happy about those comments because they made it seem as if he had been making a great deal of fuss about nothing. Despite the effects of the drug he was far from sleepy as he glared at his two companions.

'He's goin' to pay for this.'

'You let me handle it,' said Pye. 'Just get back to your job gettin' cowboys likkered up at the weekend. You're finished here.'

'He made fools of all three of us,' said Clemens. 'Him and that girl. You should arrest that uppity little cow and give her a stretch.'

'Come on,' said Pye. 'What could I arrest her for?'

'Aidin' and abettin' a criminal,' said Clemens dourly.

'Her and that father of hers,' said Jackson from the bed.

'Look, you two don't seem to realize the seriousness of the situation,' said Pye. 'If it gets out that we've been involved in an illegal attempt at a hanging and it's ever investigated by the US marshals, we'll be the ones who get put in prison.'

'They were aiding a horse thief,' said Clemens. 'You can't get away from that.'

'Listen to yourself! This Cody actually brought Mary back to her own home and handed her over to her father. He was helping her get back to her family.'

'He's a murderer.'

'Doesn't sound like the actions of a killer to me,' said Pye sourly, 'yet the widow identified him.'

'He's not our problem if we just sit here yakkin',' said Taylor. 'He'll be halfway to Tucson by now.'

'I don't think so,' said Pye thoughtfully.

'What do you mean?' asked Clemens. 'He'd be an idiot to do anything else.'

'I don't know, he seemed pretty steamed up about the fact he had been accused of murder. Perhaps there was a reason after all — besides the obvious one, I mean.'

'He ain't going to stick around,' said Clemens.

'Not unless he has a purpose.' Pye grabbed his Stetson. He checked his guns to his own satisfaction.

'Where are you goin'?' asked Clemens.

'Bud, I have a hunch that young man is going to seek revenge for what we did, and since he has to have a starting place, I'm goin' out to see Jean.'

He stomped out of the room, his spurs jangling. Normally Pye would stop for a drink or two or three, but that wasn't going to happen today.

He was a man on a mission.

5

'Don't shoot,' said Cody with a calmness that he did not feel. 'I just want to talk to you.'

'Is that why you have a weapon in your hand? Drop the durn thing then turn and face me.' He felt the pressure of the muzzle being removed from the base of his skull as she stepped back a few paces. After what had already happened to him, dropping the weapon was a hard thing to do, but he decided to obey as a token of good faith and the gun thudded to the tiled floor. He turned and slowly faced her. She was levelling a Colt .44 at him that looked ridiculously out of place in her small hands, but magnified the size of the long-barrelled firearm.

'Who are you? You're *him*.' Then she stopped and looked at him, with a long, searching gaze.

'I don't know who you think I am. You told Pye I was your husband's killer. I've never killed anyone in my life.' He felt the scar on his forehead throb as he said this, his mind searching through the haze, but he felt as if he was telling the truth.

The widow looked at him again. This time she took a step closer. He could not help noticing that she was still a good-looking woman for her age and she had a feminine scent about her that contrasted with the earthy smells he had encountered so far. 'You're not him then. You looked like him in that cell, with the light behind you and that face fungus, but it's hardly a beard at all, and that wound . . . your hair was all matted, I couldn't see the wound. Your eyes are green. His were blue, the most piercing blue I've ever seen. And you're *young*, years younger than him.'

'What are you saying?'

'I'm saying that you're not the man who killed my husband.'

'Thanks for that.' He could not keep

an ironic undertone out of his voice.

'But you're here.' She looked bewildered now. 'How could you be here? They were going to take you to the court in Tucson.'

'Is that what they told you?'

'I thought that's what they did when someone was accused of a crime as serious as murder.'

'Ma'am, you really don't know much about the rough justice in Coker Town. Out there all they care about is the business they get from the silver prospectors and the cowboys who spend their money. Justice doesn't enter into it.' He lifted his chin. 'See those burn marks on my neck? That's where they tried to hang me.'

*   *   *

Pye rode the trail out of town and went towards the ranch. His big stallion ate up the miles comfortably but did not go at any great speed. He heard the sound of hoofs rattling behind him and turned with his hand on the butt of his gun. He did not have an easy conscience. A lot of people had a grudge against him, but he was willing to use force to settle any argument, and he was the elected representative of an entire town. That was usually enough. Out here, so close to the desert, someone could settle an argument quickly enough then it would be out of sight, out of mind.

He discovered that he was being trailed by Clemens, reined back to let the liquor merchant catch up with him.

'What the hell do you want, Bud?'

'When I start a deal I finish it,' said Clemens shortly. ''Sides, if that young miscreant is out here you'll need some backup if he comes out shooting.'

'Won't be no shootin' if we do this right,' said Pye. 'OK, you can come along.'

'As if you had a choice in the matter.'

They rode on. Such was their intent on reaching the Slash T that as they got close to the building, neither man noticed a black horse in the shadow of the cottonwood trees and low bushes, still quietly cropping grass now that some of the fire had been removed from his veins.

The two men dismounted amid more cottonwoods a hundred feet from the building. Leaving their horses they made their way to the building on foot, guns at the ready, to catch the criminal who had escaped them earlier that day. Neither of them said so, but they wanted revenge for being made to look like idiots by a young man who could barely grow a beard.

* * *

A maid had approached the front room, but Jean hastily sent the girl on her way. '*Usted un favor* — leave me alone for a while.' Jean followed the girl out so that the maid would not catch a glimpse of the visitor, who had wisely concealed himself from the casual observer by standing with his back against the wall beside the door.

Jean came back shortly with a tray she carried herself on which reposed some dried beef and some green pea sauce to dip it in as well as a pitcher of water and two glasses. Cody, who hadn't thought about the matter for a while, discovered to his surprise that he was hungry.

He sat down on a padded couch with a wooden back. The couch was covered in tanned leather, and the back was richly carved with whorls and four-pointed stars carved out of the base. It had been pushed up against a wooden cabinet made from the local oak, making space to accommodate the coffin that occupied the centre of the room. Cody wasn't sure if he wanted to eat in the same room as a dead man but he couldn't see the body so ate and drank heartily while Jean sipped her own drink.

Once he had eaten he looked at her. As a man of few words he was framing his questions when she took the bull firmly by the horns.

'I know exactly what you're going to ask. Why did I identify you as a killer this very morning? Let me tell you. You looked so like him, I thought it was the same man who came in with the raiders.'

'What raiders?'

'The six of them who came here. They were led by a man called Kane, that's who I thought you were. Who are you?'

'Cody,' he replied. 'You don't seem as upset as you were earlier.'

'Well, it was a trying time for me. The sheriff said he had the man who killed my husband. When I thought it was you I crumbled. Now I have myself back under control. I feel angry, Cody, blazing angry.'

'What exactly happened?' It seemed Cody was a diffident man, but he was pressing this bereaved woman for information because he was certain that only by so doing would he find a clue as to what had happened to him just before he was attacked.

'They came to the ranch. Jake saw them coming. He said something about the Mosse gang. The one who looked like you was the obvious leader and I assumed he was Kane, though no names were given. This man had the most piercing blue eyes I have ever seen. He seemed to look through you to your very soul. Jake spoke to him straight away.'

'What did they do?'

'It was obvious when Jake started talking to him that they had known each other before. Jake spoke in a voice that was placating but firm. When the robbery was over they had all split up, leaving him with the proceeds, he said. He was just making sure the loot was being looked after while Kane was in jail. That was all, he said.'

'What loot are you talking about?'

'Gold, Cody, that's what, gold.'

'So that's what this is all about? Money?'

'Most of the world is about money,' she said sadly, 'and these men are ruthless. They don't care where it comes from.'

'But what did that have to do with your husband?'

'Don't you see, Cody? He was one of them. He had taken what they thought was rightfully theirs.'

It was then that everything began to fall into place for the young man. Jake Thatcher had come here not long ago and had bought his way into the town with his wealth.

'So he was a criminal?'

'Jake wasn't a bad person, Cody, please try to understand. He wanted away from that kind of life. He'd hidden the gold away, far away. He was a good man; he gave away a lot of money to the people of this area. He paid the ranch hands generously and well: he looked after me, got me the best of everything. Tried to settle down.'

All of this came out in a rush as the widow tried to justify what her man had done.

Cody was not too troubled by her

problems. He just wanted to understand what had happened to him so
that he could make some sense of the
world. The wound on his forehead
throbbed again; it was costing him a
great deal of effort to go on, but he
wanted to know more.

'So where does he keep the gold?'

'You, too?' She looked at him sadly.

'No, it's not like that. I don't want
your money or your gold. I just want to
know what happened.'

'They wanted to know the same
thing. They asked if he kept the gold
here, at the ranch. The thing was, Jake
was too cunning for that. He didn't
want us to be a possible target for
raiders. Most of the money was kept in
the bank in town. The main amount of
gold itself — and there's a lot of it left
— is over a hundred miles away.'

'Why?'

'Jake knew he wanted to keep his life
here separate from what he had done.
He thought I didn't know where he got
his money from originally. He always

said when he was going to get another bar to be deposited for cash, that he was going away on a 'business trip'. For a lot of men that would mean they were going away to go whoring and get drunk, but not Jake. He was going to get the means to keep us.'

'So what happened?'

'The gang held on to me while Kane shook Jake like a rat. They were going to . . . do things . . . to me in front of him to make him tell, but he went and fetched the map before they could do anything. He loved me, Cody, he would always want to keep me safe from harm.'

'So why did they kill him?'

'Jake wasn't a quitter. See that iron chest in the corner, the one with the lock on it? That's where he kept the map, but he had a gun in there too. When he brought the parchment on which it was drawn, he pulled out a pistol and drew it on Kane. Kane shot him where he stood, right in the heart. Jake was dead before he fell on his face, still clutching the map.'

'Did they . . . er . . . assault you?'

'They were going to finish the job, when a lookout shouted that Mack and a few other men were coming. While their attention was distracted I managed to run out of the door. They had their map. They loosed a few shots at me, but they had what they wanted, got their mounts and rode off across the desert.'

She looked at him thoughtfully, got up and began pacing the room, so great was her anger at what had happened to her.

'That must have been when they encountered me in the desert,' said Cody. 'I approached them . . . ' He suddenly felt consciousness slip away from his mind. When he came to he was on the ground and the woman was leaning over him with a look of concern on her fine features. He got up and shook himself like a dog shaking off water.

'I'm going to get them,' said Cody.

'Tell me where they went.'

'I can do better than that,' said Jean.

That was when they heard the thunderous knocking.

* * *

Pye was in no mood to mess around. He was tired and annoyed with this morning's work. He wanted to speak to the widow fast. He pounded the door again. Jean opened up, looking a little bewildered at his presence.

'Sam, Bud, what is it?'

'Can I come in and speak to you?'

'Well, I was busy making arrangements, but you can if you want. What's wrong?'

'The prisoner you identified just this morning is maybe around here. We need to get him because he's dangerous.'

'Why would he be here?' The widow looked bewildered.

'Because he might blame you for causing him grief and try to take his

84

revenge on you.'

'There's no one here except for myself and the maid. Reverend Service is coming over later to talk over the funeral arrangements. I don't understand, though, why you need to be here.'

'Are you sure, ma'am?' asked Clemens. 'This one is mighty bad.'

'Come in and see for yourself.' She led them into the building, carefully closing the door behind them and making a great show of bolting it into place. She led them into the airy front room. They stood in front of the coffin, both men taking off their dusty hats as a mark of respect. They both stole covert glances at the ironbound chest in the corner of the room.

'He was a good man,' said Pye. 'Now, ma'am, do you mind if we have a quick look around the place?'

'Is this really necessary?'

'As I say, this one is real dangerous.'

The two men fanned out and went through the building. They were back within a minute or two because the ranch house was not particularly large. The men stood beside the coffin again.

'Is it all right if we wait awhiles,' asked Pye, 'in case he shows up?'

'No, it isn't, Sheriff.' Jean now had a sharp tone to her voice. 'The minister is due here soon. Get out, the pair of you, please. What's it going to look like, two armed men sitting here? Besides, my own men are around.'

The two weary travellers both left the ranch, but with reluctance in every step.

'Keep your windows and doors locked,' advised Pye. 'He'll get in and try to hurt you.'

'Then maybe you should have done a better job with him.'

'He escaped with armed help. He had an accomplice. One of my deputies — Jackson Taylor — was wounded.'

'Maybe you should hire young deputies, then,' said Jean. 'Ones who can escort a prisoner the right way. Now if you'll excuse me, I have work to do.' This was her parting shot. She closed the door firmly in their faces.

'She sure is a ball breaker,' said Clemens, as they made their way back to their mounts. 'Reckon you'll have your work cut out there.'

'She's upset,' said Pye. 'Don't worry about Jean; it'll be a different story when I come to her in a few weeks when everything's settled down.'

'So, are we goin' to hang around here and wait for that rattlesnake to turn up?'

'Don't know as it would be any good. We'll take a look around the outbuildings then go. You might be right after all about him being halfway to Yuma.'

*   *   *

Back inside the house Jean waited for the men to mount their steeds, watching them from the front window, before going over to the coffin. She pulled aside the lid. Cody was inside, red-faced and bathed in sweat, his hands across his chest in the traditional manner except for the fact that he was clutching his pistol. He climbed a little stiffly out of the makeshift hiding place and stood before her, his back to one of the walls so that he could not be seen from the outside.

'Another two minutes in there and I'd have been a goner.'

'You're welcome,' she said.

'Where the hell is your husband?' She hadn't had time to explain before incarcerating him in his temporary prison.

'Jake? He's downstairs, in a wooden crate in the cellar, one of the long crates we used for transporting machinery. It's much too hot up here, while the cellar is cool and damp. I'll get my men to bring him up when the time comes.'

Cody dismissed the thought from his mind. It was not pleasant to dwell on the fact that he had been lying in what was to become a permanent residence for a man lying cold not far from where he was standing.

'You heard what those two were

saying and you still seem to trust me. Why?'

'I like Pye, though not so much his buddies, but I wouldn't trust a word they said. They're too ready to bend to public opinion. Besides, I've done you an injustice, and I owe you reparation.'

'Well, thank you. I'd best be on my way.'

'Where to?'

'I'd like to beg a little food from you, some water and a spare saddle, then I'm movin' on out.'

She looked at his glittering eyes.

'You're going to track them down, aren't you?'

'What I do once I leave here is my own business; a woman like you shouldn't be involved in this. Not any more.'

'I have a dead husband downstairs. I think this is my business more than ever. The gold is mine. I want to go there, get it, and secure the future of this ranch. There'll be no more handouts or reckless spending, just solid investment. What were you going to do?'

'I would have thought of something.'

'Like trailing this Kane, shooting him in revenge and escaping?'

'Sounds as good an idea as anything.'

She went over to the couch and reached under one of the seat cushions, pulling out a sheet of manuscript paper. 'You see this? One day I managed to get into that chest when Jake was sleeping. I took the key from around his neck and found what was so precious to him. He never knew, but I have here an exact copy of his map. Cody, I know where to get the treasure!'

★　★　★

The next day there was a sizeable crowd gathered at the Coker Town cemetery where Jake Thatcher was buried. Six cowboys brought in his coffin through the wooden arch and the open gates and carried him over to where his burial spot had already been prepared. Jean held one of the cords as they lowered him into the grave, but so did Pye, Clemens and Jackson. The latter looked distinctly uncomfortable in his role because his leg was still paining him despite the opiates he had taken earlier in the day. They had already sat through a sermon in the Northfield Baptist church where the Reverend Service had preached at length about how the good died young, to which Bud Clemens, at the back had added in a dry whisper to companions that could be the case if you were helped on your way by a good dose of lead projected at great speed.

Among the crowd was Mary, who watched the proceedings with some sadness. Jake Thatcher had been a good customer of her father, buying a lot of dry goods during the cattle-driving season. He had been short, stout and bewhiskered, looking far older than his years. Now, like Cody, he was gone.

After the ceremony, as Jean made her way to the carriage acknowledging the mourners and well-wishers as she went, Mary ran up to her just before she got into the hired coach.

'Jean, Mrs Thatcher, can I ask you, did you ever find out what happened to the young cowboy who was arrested falsely for what happened to Jake?'

'My dear young girl, I don't have a clue what you're talking about.' Jean turned on her the icy glare inherited from her Nordic ancestors.

'But he said he was going to see you.'

'Well, he was probably just saying that to an impressionable young girl. Now leave me alone; this is a sad day.'

'I'm sorry for your loss, but — '

Mary did not have a chance to complete her sentence because the carriage door was shut and Jean looked straight forward as it rode off, the forest flowers on her wide bonnet hiding her face.

Mary stood and looked at the departing vehicle with a look of stony determination on her young face. There was no doubt in her mind that the new widow had been lying through her teeth. But she had a shop to attend to and her father had made it plain he would no longer put up with her shirking any of her duties.

She was manning the store when Mack Stein came in. He was usually taciturn anyway, but this time he was like the wooden Indian that stood outside the cigar store. He simply handed her a list of dry goods and waited while — with the help of her father — she brought them together and loaded them into the wagon. Mack purchased tinned beans, molasses, sacks of maize and quite a few tools including a couple of spades and picks. The look on his face showed that he did not approve of what he was doing. When he went away, Mary, who had received no reply to her hints and probing about what it was all for, had time to think once the sales were made. It wasn't cattle-driving season — that had been a few weeks before so the desert would still be blooming. The goods Stein had bought only a short while ago were like those used by miners, but he was a ranch foreman, not a prospector. Besides, his employer had financed the purchase. There was only one conclusion to draw from the business: *someone* at the Slash T was going on an expedition in the very near future and it didn't take much in the way of thinking to decide that it was going to be Jean herself. She would need help with something like that, and who better than a young man who was getting fitter by the day as he recovered from his ordeal in the desert?

By now it was too late to check, but Mary lifted her firm chin as she decided that early the next day she was going to ride out to the Slash T with a few supplies just in case her hunch was right.

* * *

It was the night before they were going to leave. They were both in the ranch

94

house, the space lit by the steady glow of oil lamps. Cody was fresh and rested and eager to depart.

'Every day we wait allows them to get to the gold,' he said. 'It's lodged — where did you say?'

'Bear Canyon, about a hundred miles south across the desert,' said Jean. 'I've never been there myself but it looks fairly easy to get to, a couple of days at the most.'

'I don't think you should go,' said Cody.

'Why not?'

'You loaded the weapons and ammo yourself. We're going into a dangerous situation. Besides, I've heard rumours that some of the Indians are kicking up at being held in the reservation over in the hills. I hear they're looking to take their revenge on any white expedition they come across.'

'Rumours,' said Jean. 'Who needs them?'

'I heard a rumour about the Mosse gang,' said Cody, 'that's why I'm here.'

He stopped, surprised by what he had just said. Then he felt the pain in his head rise and hastily retreated from any more thoughts on that particular subject. It was obvious that along with the wound on his forehead, he was healing on the inside too.

'Cody, it's not that I don't trust you, but Jake was going to go there with some of our men anyway; now that he's dead it's time for me to take charge.'

That ended it. Yet neither of them got much sleep that night.

6

The wagon was fully loaded and prepared the next morning. Mack Stein had learned that Cody was in the building by then. He had not been back to town and so had not heard the rumours that the cowboy had escaped from custody. Even so, on meeting the young man, Mack had stared at the scar on his forehead. He had been incredulous when Jean had told him that they were going on a trip together 'to do some cattle business', as she so blatantly informed him, and that Mr Brown (as she called Cody) was a representative of the Western Stock company. They would be back, she told him, in a few days.

The trouble with this viewpoint was that Mack knew full well what was going on. He had been with Jake on two previous trips — only the two of them

— and he knew full well that you didn't provision yourself for a journey of more than a week just to look at breeding stock in another town. Jake had always completed the final part of the trip himself, had always come back in triumph with a full saddle-bag, told his employee nothing, returned, and started to spend again. Mack had a shrewd idea of what Jake was doing. Once or twice the foreman had been tempted to take over and make some money, but why kill the goose that literally laid the golden egg? Jake had been generous enough. Mack had been in trouble with the law in the past and at his age he didn't want to start all that again. Let Jake take the burden for his own actions.

This put a different spin on the matter, though. Mack did not like the way the new widow was going about her business. The fact that she had trusted some upstart with her business, rather than a man who knew what he was doing, deeply troubled him.

'I'm leaving you in charge,' said Jean, 'have a couple of men make sure the property is protected all the time. Thanks, Mack, you're my rock in these hard times.'

He smiled at her sourly, but since this was no different from his expression at other times she did not notice. After the wagon had gone in a flurry of dust — the young man riding the coal-black stallion beside the pair of dappled mares — Mack walked back into the building vacated by his employer. In the airy front room was a shelf on which she kept all her spirits, including fine brandies. He lifted a bottle of cognac, uncorked it and began to drink steadily.

* * *

Cody, who had eaten a full breakfast of eggs and flat bread, washed down with about a gallon of coffee, felt well, better than ever as they rode out towards the desert. They had set out early for a simple reason: the heat of the day would rise steadily. From midday onwards it would be bad for the horses — and them — to ride in the heat. They would find a bluff of rock that made deep shadows and shelter there for a few hours until the heat had abated. The horses were vital in this expedition and they could not risk them suffering from sunstroke.

'Pity I'm still a horse-thief,' he said to her, as he prepared his stallion with the saddle and bridle she had provided. 'Maybe you can supply me with another and let Jackson have this one back.'

'Don't bother,' she said briefly. 'This is *my* horse.'

'What?'

'He was being stabled in town. Jackson was thinking of buying him. He was using him without my permission that day, for legitimate business, at least that's what he told me. If he tries to get you as a horse-thief I'll get *him* for being one and then we'll see who gets hanged.'

They rode steadily throughout the morning. Out here, where there was scrubland, the big saguaros, dried-out looking mesquite bushes and low desert flowers, with only the yip of the odd coyote or desert fox for company, Cody seemed to come into his own; he looked more at home in this vast red landscape than he had ever done before. He guided them to their first stop beside a big line of boulders taller than a three-storey house, and they gratefully drank water while Jean spread out the map on the ground.

'Where are we?' she asked.

' 'Bout twenty miles on from where we started,' said Cody. 'Trouble is the trail petered out real soon and we had to make our way across the desert itself.' It was his turn to confront her.

'You can go back. There's still time. I'll take some canteens and ride on. Reckon I could be there within the day if I was alone.'

'Why would you do that?'

'It's all right, you can keep your map.

I ain't interested. All I want to do is get hold of them miscreants and make sure they get what's due to them, especially that leader of theirs. I'm guessing it's him who left me in this state, ready to die. I'll make sure they never touch another innocent man.'

'There's six of them,' said Jean. 'You'll be biting off more than you can chew.'

'Really? Tell me, Jean, you're the only other person here, what good are the two of us going to be?'

'Is this because I'm a woman?'

'Hell, no, well, maybe a little.' He looked confused at his own words.

'If we get there we'll hide and pick them off,' said Jean. 'I can hold them down and cover while you do what you want to do — then we'll get the gold and go.'

'Can you even shoot?'

She did not answer him but casually picked up a gun and aimed at a passing lizard about thirty feet away. The shot rang out loud in the empty landscape and the lizard was no more.

'Does that answer your question?'

'I guess so.'

'They might not even be there. The gold might be gone.'

'Sure, but what else can we do?'

The cry of a coyote in the distance filled the silence between them as his question went unanswered.

* * *

Mary rode up to the Slash T feeling a little nervous. What if her instinct was wrong about what had happened and he wasn't here? Then she braced herself. She would rather be left with a substantial amount of egg over her facial features than miss out on facing the hated Cody. She was barely forty feet from the ranch when a burly figure came out with a shotgun in his hand and fired a warning salvo into the soil barely three feet from where she rode, making her horse rear in the air.

'All right, mister, get away from here

real fast,' said Mack. She realized that in her dark trousers and wide-brimmed hat along with her check shirt and short coat, she probably did look as if she was some indeterminate character from a distance.

'Mack, it's me,' she called.

'Miss Mary?' he said thickly, putting the shotgun aside. 'What the hell?'

'What's going on? This isn't the kind of welcome you usually give your visitors,' she said, as she dismounted and moved towards the disgruntled foreman. She could tell, as she got closer, that he was furious at something. The sight of a supposed stranger had pushed him over the edge. The fumes coming from him also made her hope that he did not light a match in the next five seconds or they would both go up in smoke.

'What happened?'

'He's gone with her,' said Mack.

'Who has?'

'Don't rightly know his name. Gordy, I think,' mumbled the foreman. 'Her a widow not a week and she's off with him.'

'Where have they gone?' asked Mary, feeling a thrill of discovery. She had been right after all.

'Out there, into the desert,' said Mack *in vino veritas*. 'They think I'm a fool, that I don't know where they're heading. Bear Canyon, that's where.'

'Where's that?' asked Mary.

'Southwards,' said Mack. 'Up towards them big caves.'

Mary had heard of the caves that had belonged to the Pueblo Indians, inhabitants of this region for hundreds, if not thousands of years.

'I'm going to get them,' she said. 'Thanks, Mr Stein. Just one more thing, did he make her go with him?'

Mack stared at her and the madness that came from the alcohol spread through his brain. A slow smile spread across his face.

'Yeah, I guess you could say that, he had some kind of hold over her.'

'That's enough for me.' Mary spurred

her horse into action and soon she was on their trail. Like most of her ilk — riders who had been doing so since birth — she was able to tell which direction she going by the sun, and when that vanished, by the stars at night, so she was able to follow them with comparative ease. Also, since they quickly went off the beaten track they left some distinct marks.

This, and the fact that she was barely an hour behind them, meant that soon she was riding into view of the couple sheltering in the shadows of the red rocks.

* * *

Cody was the first to see her. Like Mack before him it was hard to tell whether the figure was a man or a woman. He leapt to his feet. Jean had provided him with a pair of good Colt pistols and he pulled both of these out, readying himself for a possible assault from the new arrival. Instead what happened was anti-climactic. Dabs slowly made her way towards where Cody stood, no doubt recognizing in him some kind of authority over horses. The figure wearing the wide-brimmed hat, who had been riding in the full, blazing heat of the sun, swayed in the saddle then slid forward and off the horse, hat falling to the ground as it did so, revealing the long copper locks that belonged to the girl.

After getting her and the animal into shadow Jean gave her water and let her revive in her own time. Cody was tight-lipped with fury and could not be restrained once he saw the girl was up and about.

'Do you know what the hell you're doing?'

'I came to stop you hurting any more people.'

'What in the Blue Hills are you talking about? I'm the one only here who has been harmed. Look at this wound. Do you think I did this to myself?'

'I don't care, you seem to cause havoc wherever you go.' The girl was facing him now, her hands on her hips. 'Jean, he's trouble. He'll get you killed.'

'You get out of here,' he said. 'When it's safe, you just get on your horse and ride right out of here. Go back to your daddy and your store, missy.'

'Don't order me about. I'll do what I want.'

'You're not wanted here. Get that through your head. You'll go all right.'

Then Cody remembered the warnings he himself had made about the renegade Indians to Jean just a short while ago. The girl might have been lucky once, but if the Chiricahua really were on the warpath it would just take one encounter for her to die a bloody death. Before they killed her they would defile her in ways he didn't even want to think about. His head wound throbbed as it always did when he tried to think about any past knowledge. All he knew was that they didn't have time to go back for all sorts of reasons, one of which was that the sheriff might still be gunning for him with his pet deputies, but the other, more pressing to his mind, being that the Mosse gang with a couple of days' lead would already have the gold and be on their way. If they had moved on he had vowed to track them down, leaving Jean camped safely at the canyon until his return.

'You'll have to come with us,' he said. 'We don't have the time to get you back home. Did you know that some Indians are supposed to have gone missing from their reservation in the hills? They could be anywhere in this region. As if there ain't enough problems with crossing a desert, we've got them to contend with.'

'I'm all right. I can do what I need to do,' said the girl. 'Just give me a gun and I'll do the rest.'

'You ain't getting a gun, that's for sure,' said Cody. 'You look mean enough to use it on us.'

'Why exactly are you here, child?' asked Jean. This was the wrong question to ask the girl. She stalked away and sat by herself not talking to either of them for a long time.

'You know I heard that Bear Canyon itself was a sacred place to the Apaches,' said Jean. 'Apparently some black bears had managed to get down from the hills, living and breeding in the area for hundreds of years. Some tribes hunt bears but worship them too for their strength and cunning.'

'So what you're saying is that it makes sense for them to be around here? The Apaches, I mean, not the bears?'

'Yes.'

They settled down until the heat had begun to dissipate. It was late afternoon by that time and they still had a great distance to go on a faint, almost unused trail. They couldn't hurry the wagon too much because the wheels were made of wood, and even if protected by metal, they could still snap if a deep rift in the stony ground strained the axle beyond endurance. Then they really would be in trouble.

Cody had other worries to think about as they made their way. The girl was a competent enough rider as she showed in the steady movement of her mount across the rugged plain, but it was not her he was worried about at this particular moment.

He thought he had seen a wisp of smoke in the distance. That could be the campfire of the cowboys who had killed Jake, making their way back towards the border after getting in and taking the gold. Worse still, it could be the renegades they had been discussing earlier.

They made good progress as the long day wore on; Cody finally brought them to a halt in a large gully when the sun was starting to go down.

'No use going any further. We're already about halfway there. Unfetter the horses and we'll strike camp.' It was amazing, but this unassuming young man, who only two days before had been languishing in a prison cell awaiting his hanging, had assumed a mantle of authority. The other two obeyed him. The horses made what they could of the local scrub — no lush meadows around here — augmented by some of the oats stored in the wagon. It was axiomatic out here that you looked after your beast before yourself because that could be the best way to survive. They set up camp and burned some of the dried-out wood they found lying around. This was not a place often frequented by either natives or cattle merchants because it was of no commercial interest or sacred significance whatsoever. They cooked and ate their food.

'Are you going to tell me why we're here?' asked Mary.

'I've already asked you the same thing,' said Jean. It was plain that the two women were not going to get on with each other.

'The less you know, the less trouble you can get into,' said Cody.

'You're treating me like a child again.'

'I didn't ask you to come here.'

'Know what? Tomorrow I'm getting right on Dabs and going back the way I came.'

'I would let you if I didn't think they would find your bones in the desert after six weeks. The foxes and buzzards would pick you clean in no time.'

'You're infuriating.'

'You said it.' Even in the faint glow of the firelight the livid wound on his forehead could be seen.

'You're impossible.'

The girl stamped off to the canvas shelter they had brought with them. Jean looked at Cody across the fire. They had built it some distance from the wagon for fear that a stray ember might set it alight, and the shelter was beside the wagon.

'You do know,' she said softly, 'that girl, well, she's here purely because of you?' The way she said it indicated something else he didn't want to examine.

Cody wriggled as if someone had put insects down his shirt. He kicked dirt

113

on to the fire and stood up, all but invisible in the starlight.

'I'm going to turn in,' he said stiffly, waiting for her. Jean had elected to sleep in the wagon while Cody rolled in his blankets, head pillowed on a saddle-bag, and lay beneath the vehicle.

He awoke to find the first threads of dawn trailing into the gully. Two concerned faces were looking at him. He had also rolled into the open. He got up stiffly, testing his limbs. The wound on his forehead was throbbing painfully again.

'You were having some kind of nightmare,' said Jean.

'You were shouting about leaving home and begging someone not to kill you,' added Mary.

'You said you had a reason for that request,' said Jean. 'Then you woke up screaming.'

He looked at them blankly.

'Let's get somethin' to eat and get movin',' was all he had to say.

They made their preparations. Cody

was careful to inspect the wheels of the wagon. They were showing some sign of wear and tear already, but looked as if they would be able to get them there and back. Hopefully by that time they would be carrying more than just food or water. He had come round to Jean's way of thinking that this was to be more than just a bloodletting mission. He was essentially a man of peace. The best way of remembering the generous benefactor of a town was to outgun those who would take away the fount of that generosity.

The man and the girl were about to mount their horses, when they heard one of the most blood-curdling sounds a white settler could hear.

It was the wild whoop of Apaches on the warpath. Right at that second they were thundering down the gully on captured horses, riding fast towards the small party, painted, seated on woven blankets for saddles, wearing head-dresses of eagle feathers, and ready for slaughter.

7

'Where is that girl?' asked Donald Sutton. Mary was proving to be a trouble to him, just when he was getting more business from hopeful silver prospectors who were trekking into the area after news that a big new vein had been discovered on unclaimed land. If you could stake a claim quickly you could get rich quickly too. Most of those who tried failed to get any reward. In the meantime, Donald benefited because they bought equipment and dry goods from him, which they needed whether they succeeded or not.

'I don't know.' Elizabeth seemed genuinely worried. 'This thing with the Cody boy seems to have gone too far. Wait, is her horse still here?'

Her father, cursing under his breath, walked over to the livery, which was just down the street. Old Tom, who tended the horses, gave him the bad news.

'Yep, the young lady rode out real early this morning, 'bout an hour ago. I figured you had given her a job to do. You keep her busy, that I'll say.'

'Did she have any supplies with her?'

'Yep, plenty of food and water. She was well wrapped up too against the morning air. Muttering to herself too, she was, a mite angry. I heard her say something to herself about the Slash T.'

'Thanks, Tom.'

Donald did not say anything else. He went back to the hardware store and told Elizabeth that he knew where their daughter had gone. He quickly settled his business, donned his riding clothes and equipped himself with a gun, then called Billy forward. He knelt down on one knee.

'Son, you're a good boy.'

'You don't always say that, Pop; the other day when I climbed up the — '

'Never mind that.'

'You swore you would paddle me

good next time.'

'Forget that,' said Donald between gritted teeth. 'I have to go now, son. I might be gone for a little while. You look after your mother. Help her out in the store. You understand?'

Billy nodded with unnecessary vigour.

'All right.' Donald gave him a jovial punch on the upper arm then stood up and held his wife.

'Goodbye, dear.' He gave her an affectionate kiss.

He went over to the stables, and mounted the gelding he also kept there.

'Ructions, is it?' asked Old Tom, but Donald was already on his way by then.

As he made his way towards the ranch he was surprised to hear that he had company. He reined in his steed and found that three angry-looking men, namely the sheriff and his two unpaid deputies, were trailing him. It looked as though Jackson had recovered from his wound.

'Whoa, what is it?' asked Donald.

'I'm in a hurry.'

'I've heard rumours that you've been sellin' supplies to the Slash T,' said Pye bluntly.

'So what? They buy supplies off me all the time.'

'These ones were different. Seems someone's going on a little trip.'

'Never thought about it.' In truth he hadn't, people were always going on the trail. When there was no railway it was the only way to go any distance.

'I saw your girl ridin' out of here this mornin',' said Jackson sourly. 'Looked as if she was on a little expedition of her own. I'd have got after her quicker too if this fat buzzard had got his carcass into gear sooner. Care to enlighten us, Donald?'

'Look, I don't know what you've heard, or indeed what has happened. All I know is that she's gone and this is my only clue.'

'If you don't know, why are you all tooled up?' asked Pye.

'I'm just well prepared.'

'So are we,' said the sheriff.

There was nothing more to discuss so they rode past the hanging tree, the meadows and woods until they came to the ranch. They wisely halted their mounts and approached on foot, dodging through the sagebrush and trees until they were close to the building. Donald elected to approach the front. He had a personal stake in this. He battered on the door with the butt of his gun.

'Mary, are you in there?'

But the door swung open as if operated by a ghost. Donald stepped inside, not knowing what to find, but it was certainly not the heap of a dark body in the front room, nor the frightened servant girl who squeaked out of his way as he entered.

'Eet has nothing to do with me,' she gasped.

'It's all right, leave us alone.' As Donald moved forward the other three joined him, crowding into the ranch house. Pye came forward and kicked the heap in the centre of the main room.

'Mack, what the hell are you doing?'

Donald had feared that the man was dead, but he gave a groan when Pye's boot made contact with his ribs.

'Damn cow,' he said, trying to get up, staggered and fell on his backside.

'What happened? Where's my daughter?' asked Donald. 'Have they kidnapped her?'

Mack looked at him blearily.

'Mistah Shutton?' The words were slurred. 'That damn scheming cow, that bashtard. They've taken her.' He narrowed his eyes. 'Out there. She's hoshtage all right, out to Bear Canyon.' This was about as much effort as he could make. He flopped on his back and began snoring again.

At the words 'Bear Canyon' Pye gave a start.

'We've got to go after them,' said Donald. 'If we ride hard we can catch up with her.'

'You'd be a goddam fool to go out

there in the desert without supplies,' said Pye. 'Still, gives me an idea.'

He fetched the frightened maid and asked her for some details about what she had seen. The girl, Rosita, hadn't seen Mary because she had been keeping away from Mack, who had groped her a few times on the sly, but she showed them to an outbuilding where the spare supplies were kept.

'I agree with you, Sutton,' said Pye. 'That fugitive's out there with my prospective wife — though she doesn't know it yet — and your girl. He could do anythin'. Nothin' like the present. We'll load up an' ship out.'

Donald was in his early middle years. He was used to his home comforts, a warm bed, a good cigar and a glass of whiskey before bed. He worked long hours in the store, especially when there was a rush on like today, and he felt he was entitled to these things. However, he was also a veteran of the Civil War. He had been quite young when the war started, but they were recruiting and not asking too many questions. He had fought on the Confederate side and, after the war, had experienced plenty of hardship, so he was not a man who was unaware of the situation he was getting himself into. He was also used to being prepared and it was he who made sure that they would be carrying enough food and water, fairly divided between them, to survive the trip.

While Donald was getting the horses ready, with some help from the servant girl, his two companions in the ranch bearded Pye, and from the looks on their faces he knew they wanted some answers fast.

'What in the name of Sam Hill are you up to, Pye?' asked Jackson.

'I want to see justice done,' said Pye.

'We know you,' said Clemens bluntly. 'That girl, she's outa your jurisdiction now, trailing her britches halfway across a desert. If you didn't need to go after her, you wouldn't bother.'

'That widow is mine now,' said Pye.

'Despite her upset the other day, I think she knows it.'

'That ain't the reason either,' said Jackson. 'She's a good-lookin' woman all right, but you can get your needs in the whorehouse an' you often do. If she vanishes without issue the county court'll make a judgment about the ranch an' put it up to the highest bidder, which could be you. So I ask you, Sammy, what are you up to?'

'I'm going after the source of Jake's wealth,' said Pye. 'That good enough for you two filibusters?'

'Good enough for me,' said Bud. As a storekeeper who made a reasonable living, but who had some taste for gambling and the high life, this was a quest that made sense to him.

'Now, are you two merchants goin' to get sworn in as my legal deputies in front of Sutton so we can get this done?'

In ordinary circumstances neither of the men would have joined the sheriff in what they would have termed 'a darned fool quest', but this was before they had learned what he was really up to. Now neither of them wanted him to become wealthy at their expense if he got to the widow before they did. Neither of them thought too hard about what it was really going to be like out in the heat of the Sonora desert. Besides, it was still early, they might catch up with the girl and Jean before the end of the day.

After being sworn in, they saddled up and rode across the desert. Except for Donald, none of them had any experience of riding this way and they pushed their horses a little too hard. By early afternoon it was becoming apparent that they would have to rest whether they wanted to or not. Fortunately the landscape was so rugged it was easy for them to find a place in which to shelter. The desert was full of such dips in the ground, sheltered by the tall mesas.

'Don't know whether I should have told you, boys,' said Pye, 'but there's a rumour that some of them child-like savages are on the go again.'

'Indians?' Clemens looked as if he had gulped down a draught of poisoned liquor.

'They can't be,' said Jackson, 'I heard they was caught up in a reservation in the Colorado hills.'

'Yeah, well, some of the younger ones ain't happy with their tribal elders,' said Pye. 'They reckon they've been hard done by. They're Chiricahuas, and they can get pretty worked up about things like their ancestral lands.'

'Well, they had the land for long enough,' said Jackson, 'an' they did nothing with it, so it's only right it goes to men who can make something of the place.'

'I ain't here to argue about the politics of the thing,' said Pye. 'Just keep a lookout for any hotheads an' be ready for a fight.' He did not look all that displeased with the idea.

'I'll be ready for them,' said Donald, 'if it comes to a fight.' He had such a fierce look on his normally placid face that the other three fell silent for a moment. Here was a man who was ready and prepared to battle for what he believed in.

'I think we should go back,' said Clemens, 'never mind the money. Fighting savages was never part of the deal.'

'What money?' demanded Donald. There was an uncomfortable silence.

'He means the reward we'll get for helping Jean,' said Jackson. You had to be quick-witted if you were a saloon owner.

'Bud, you're welcome to ride back,' said Pye. 'Give my love to the town — oh, and tell them all you abandoned the search for a wanted killer.'

They rode on later in the afternoon. By this time there was an uncomfortable silence between the men. Donald just wanted to rescue his daughter, and now he had the added fear that she might encounter Indians. Pye wanted to catch up with the widow and the other two no longer wanted to be there given that neither of them really enjoyed fighting, unless the battle was rigged. Fighting was for men like the sheriff.

Once more the desert defeated them. Once or twice they had been forced on a particular path, but that had been to their benefit when they saw clear signs that others had been there before them.

'I think we're near them,' said Pye. 'Let's get settled for the night. If we get up early we can catch up in an hour or less, is what I'm guessin'.'

His two new deputies were not used to sleeping in the open and moaned and groaned and complained about the cold.

'Quit your whinin'. Save your energy for sleep,' snapped Pye. Soon they were silent too and the night wore on.

Donald was the first up the next morning. He woke the other three. The air was still cold and the sun was barely lifting over the horizon.

'Come on, do what you have to do and let's get going.' As a veteran he knew the tactical worth of stealing a march on your enemy. Not that the women were his opponents, but Cody was not his favourite person at the moment. If they could catch up with the three perhaps they could get rid of the young man and get back to the town before nightfall.

The others roundly cursed him, but Pye realized that Donald was right in what he was doing. They were all refreshed and started to ride as hard as they could over the desert, taking the route that must have been followed by the wagon, still picking up traces on the way until they came to the valley where their targets had rested the previous night.

They saw the wagon in the distance accompanied by the lone horseman on his big black mount, for it was a clear area, but even as they arrived, blood-curdling yells could be heard from the other side. Not half a mile away, their screams echoing off the high sides of the valley came the men looking to take the lives of the upstart settlers.

8

The Indians were attacking just as the sun was rising in the sky and the air was still cool. Their whoops echoed and rebounded off the walls. Not for them the silent attack on what they saw as the enemy, but a proud declaration of who they were and what they were going to do. Cody could not have said how many were in the party as they poured into the valley, certainly fifteen or so. More than enough to overwhelm their small group, that was a certainty. Most of the Indians were armed with spears, war axes or bows and arrows. This was no accident, since the white man's government had managed to take away most of the weapons they had traded in earlier years when the tribes were moved to their reservations. These were young men making a stand against what they saw as the desecration of their rights, and no one was safe from them as they stood up for what they believed in.

Of course the three travellers looked on the situation in a different way. Cody did not have time to think, which is often the best way in dire situations such as the one they were facing. He leaped from the back of his horse, wrested the reins away from Jean and urged the wagon round, then he released the animals. Jean watched in disbelief as the wagon cambered to one side.

There was a reason behind this seemingly suicidal act. He knew full well that if he waited for Jean to mount his horse, and the three of them fled on two horses, the tribesmen would soon catch up with them and dispatch them with their weapons. Fleeing from the scene was not the option it would have been if they had been given more warning.

'You two shelter behind the wagon,' he yelled at the women. 'Don't try and run.' The warriors were getting close by then and arrows thudded into the woodwork at the front of the wagon, just missing the widow. Hastily she climbed down, taking shelter as advised. Mary looked as if she was going to stay on her horse and defy them with her one gun, but Cody grabbed her right leg, pulled her down and thrust her over to where Jean was sheltering. The wagon had keeled over on its side, acting as a barrier. This was their one chance.

Cody had a six-shooter in each hand. He stood up quickly and loosed off a few rounds. His bullets did not miss their mark. The trouble for the Indians was that only one or two of them were armed, and arrows fired from the back of a horse had a way of going just wide. Cody knew in his heart, the wound on his head throbbing fiercely as the thought reached his mind, that they were probably all going to die, but he was not going to go down without a fight. If it came to it he would shoot both the women himself to spare them the indignities that would be heaped upon them by the tribesmen. They reserved a special torture for white women, raping them first then inflicting cuts on them and leaving them staked to the ground to be eaten by wildlife, or to die in agonizing thirst in the hot sun.

He showed that he was a stunningly accurate marksman, hitting six men with his six shots, clearly killing at least two of them, badly disabling the others. This, of course, did not discourage the rest. They would fight to the last man; it was one of the things that had made the Apaches such a difficult enemy for the authorities. Even as he emptied his gun, he threw it to Jean for her to reload.

Then he found a slim, darkly clad figure by his side. Mary fired without hesitation, taking out two of the warriors in short order. He would have admired her marksmanship if it hadn't been for the dire danger they still faced. The remaining Indians had dismounted and were still whooping and screaming fiercely as they came towards the fallen wagon. At least six remained, more than enough to finish off the three. The warriors scrambled over the wagon. Cody closed at open quarters with the Indian, dodging the descent of a club that would have knocked his brains out, and shooting the man in the face at point-blank range.

From the corner of his eye Cody could see that Jean was lying on her back, about to be speared. She had a gun in her hand but did not have the time to aim. He seized the fallen man's club and smashed Jean's attacker on the back of the head. The warrior, already dead, fell on top of the recumbent woman. This actually saved her life, because the other attackers scrambled over their dead comrade and made straight for their main enemy: Cody.

He felt a sickening blow as a club crashed into his right shoulder. Mary was pulled away from him and he saw her struggling between two of the Indians. He knew what they would do with her once he was dead and redoubled his efforts to fight against his new assailant, an Indian about his own age, only this man was fiercely painted with red and yellow paint on his cheeks and chin and black soot smudges under his eyes to make them bigger and more terrifying. He was armed with an axe in one hand and the club that had inflicted the crushing blow with the other.

Cody managed to duck and avoid a sweeping swing of the axe that would have taken off the top of his head, but he had fallen with his back to the wagon. His guns were both empty now.

'Ayyia!' With a wild cry of exultation the young Indian raised his axe to cleave Cody's skull in two. There was the crack of a pistol and the Indian cried out in agony as the shot went straight through his back and out of his chest, spattering Cody with his life-blood. Cody saw four men ride forward, recognizing three of them immediately as those who did not have his best interests at heart.

The Indians holding Mary let go of her, picked up their clubs and spears then sprang at the new enemy. They were soon dispatched with bullets straight to the heart, fired by Pye, who had no problem targeting them.

The valley was now littered with the dead bodies of the warriors, not one of whom had survived, since those with injuries quickly expired. Cody slumped forward in a dead faint as the injury overwhelmed him.

When he awoke he was still aware of the pain in his shoulder, lying in the shelter of the heeled-over wagon. He tried to move his right arm, discovering that although it was painful to do so, he was still able to move the fingers of his hand. He worked the shoulder back and forth, feeling fresh spasms of pain, but knowing that if he did not do so the muscles would stiffen and he would be unable to use that arm for a while. As he did this he glared at the new arrivals. The sheriff still had his gun in his hand, but this time it was pointed in Cody's direction.

The new arrivals were still looking around, wary that other warriors might be in the region.

'Looks as if this is them all,' said Pye. 'Painted savages.' He kicked one of the bodies. 'You,' he said to Cody. 'You're under arrest for a whole bunch of offences.'

'Leave him alone.' Jean was dusty, still smeared in blood from the attack. 'He saved our lives!'

'We can't go on anyway,' said Cody reasonably, ignoring the pain in his limb, 'there might be more of them out there. As for you,' he said, glaring at the sheriff, 'you don't have any jurisdiction over me out here.'

Pye scowled and raised his gun, pointing it straight at Cody's heart.

'I figure one more dead maverick won't make no headlines,' he said.

'Leave him alone!' roared Donald, thrusting himself between the sheriff and the young man who had just managed to stand up. Mary came forward and stood beside Cody.

'Shoot him and you shoot me,' she warned. Reluctantly Pye put his gun back into its holster.

'You can't escape the law forever, son. Despite the way you fooled the widow I know you just ain't right. They say you cain't remember what happened to you: I reckon that's just some story to lead us on. I'll be keepin' an eye on you this whole trip.'

'I got a personal grudge,' said Taylor Jackson. 'You got me shot, boy. The sheriff might be more forgiving, but if I get you alone we'll settle the score over my leg.'

'I was the one shot you,' said Mary. 'If I had the choice, next time it would be your stupid brains I would send flying out of your head.'

'Now, Mary.' Donald cast his daughter a warning look.

'Let's clear away these poor men,' said Jean. She was sad to see so many young, dead warriors, despite the fact that they would have shown her no mercy and that by the end of their tortures she would have been begging for a death they would not have given her.

The rest of the party set to work. It was a narrow valley, already littered with rocks, and they had to clear the bodies so they could go on their way. For Donald, as a veteran, it was no great task. He had seen sights just as bad, or worse, in the old days, but he was worried about his daughter. After the bodies were cleared away and hidden as best they could, in case others came this way, the party gathered and righted the wagon.

The horses belonging to the warriors had fled clean away. They were semi-wild anyway and would make for some kind of pasture. Those belonging to Mary and Jean, along with Satan, had retreated to the other end of the valley.

Cody had done his share of clearing up the bodies with the rest, assisting

Mary. He was still smarting under the insults from Pye which had labelled him a pariah and a criminal. Worse still, there was a lurking thought in the back of his mind that the lawman might be right. Maybe he, Cody, had been doing an unlawful act. Perhaps he had even been part of the Mosse gang who had killed Jake, albeit one Jean had never seen. After all, she had said not long ago that there had been a lookout. Maybe he was that man. But then, if that was the case, why had they attacked him?

Cody knew somehow that this was probably not the case, that when he had been left for dead there was another reason, but the nagging feeling would not leave him. He could not be entirely sure. At least if he was a criminal he would have known what to do, namely protest his innocence and get away from the rest as fast as possible.

Now that things had been restored to comparative normality, it was still early on in the day. There was still a distinct chill in the air. Cody was the first to speak about the matter as he looked at the low sun.

'Once we get out of here, the going ain't too bad. I reckon we could get most of the ways before the afternoon. My advice would be to turn back after this, but it's up to you folks.'

'Reckon the pup's got his head screwed on in some ways,' said Pye. 'I say we go for it.'

'We've got my daughter, which is all that counts,' said Donald. 'I think we should turn back.'

'We'll divide the party up,' said Jean. 'You go back with your daughter, we'll go and finish our task. Take Pye and his cronies with you. We'll be all right; like you say, if we go hard at it we should get there soon.'

'I told you, this miscreant ain't leaving my sight,' said Pye. 'Jean, I'm sorry you fell in with someone so crooked.'

'Well,' said Donald, sweeping his gaze over the other two men, 'are you going to escort us back to Coker Town?'

'Not me,' said Jackson. 'Give me the choice I'll stay with the two best-armed folks. Besides, Pye is up to somethin' an' I aim to find out what if it involves money.'

'I'm not going over that rough country with a young girl an' her dad,' said Clemens. 'Am stickin' with the boss here.'

'Then you leave us no choice. Come on, Mary, we'll load up with supplies, as they've been saying; if we ride hard for a day we'll be at least on the edge of town.'

'I'm not going, Father.' Mary stayed glued to the spot.

'What?'

'These men don't have Cody's best interests at heart, or even those of Jean. If we leave them to it, he'll never stand trial anywhere because he'll be dead.'

'Mary,' said Cody, 'you don't get this. I can handle myself. You saw what we did to those Indians.' He was not being proud of the fact, merely telling the truth. 'Go back with your father. I want you to do it for your own sake. We don't know what other dangers we might have to face. I don't want you to get hurt.'

The girl looked at him and saw that he was telling the simple truth. He wasn't shouting at her or haranguing her, just being straightforward. She turned calmly to her father.

'Daddy, I'm not going back. I've come this far. I want to be with Jean and Cody and do what I can.'

'Mary, you'll get on that horse and come with me.' For the first time since shooting the tribesmen who had held his daughter prisoner, Donald showed serious signs of anger. 'I promised your mother I would look after you. I don't call letting you get into this foolhardy quest a fair way of doing that very thing. You're not too old to paddle, you know.'

'Wait,' said Cody, 'if you go back you can take Satan. He's big an' real fast.'

'You forget that horse ain't yours to

143

give,' said Jackson peevishly.

'He ain't yours either,' said Cody. 'Is it a deal, Mary?'

'I'm going on.' She lifted the firm chin she had inherited from her father.

'While we're standing here arguing we're using up time that could get us to the settlement,' said Jean.

'What settlement?' asked Cody.

'There's a small farming village out at Bear Canyon,' said Jean. 'It was established a few years ago. They've got everything we might need for the return journey. Food, water, supplies. We can trade these tools with them once we're finished doing what we're going to do.'

Donald looked at her with a puzzled expression.

'What exactly are you going to do?'

'Find Jake's gold,' said the widow. 'He owed me that much after I stood by him, even when I knew what he must have done.'

Now that it was in the open there a palpable tension in the group. Donald now knew that the men who had accompanied him, far from wanting to help a friend, were out to help themselves.

'Mary, I don't want you mixed up in this.' He looked at his daughter.

'Sorry, I have to go.' The girl did not even look at Cody as she spoke, but he knew that she was still looking out for him. With a sigh of resignation Donald reined in his horse.

'What are we waiting for? I just hope we don't attract any more savages.'

The horses rode onwards, with Cody and Mary flanking the wagon as it went through the low sagebrush and skirted the giant saguaros and dead-looking Joshua trees that would spring into bloom once the rains came. The two young people kept a lookout for Jean as she drove her pair along, stopping her several times from driving into breaks in the rocks that would almost certainly have damaged one or more of her wheels, making the wagon unfit for purpose. However, because they had started so early, and avoided any accidents on the rough terrain, they were able to cover a considerable number of miles before they had to stop in another long, sheltered gully, where they were able to keep out of the midday sun.

'Reckon we could get that son of a rattlesnake now,' said Pye. 'Ask him to step back for a word or two, start yellin' that he's attackin' us then shoot out his fool brains. Easy enough to do. Self-defence. The girl wouldn't buy it, but who cares?'

'Well, you're doin' it on your own,' said Jackson. 'Didn't you see what he did over in that cursed valley? He killed most of them before we even came on the scene. That kid's a rip-roarin' gun-fighter.'

'It's all right,' said Pye comfortably, 'I can bide my time. Just an idea, that's all.'

Soon it was time for them to be on the move. They had to make their way around a particularly tall and wide outcrop of red rock at the end, but what they saw was worth the trip. There, lying below them on a slope they would have to take carefully on their horses, lay Bear Canyon.

After so much scrubland and desert the area was a shock. Bear Canyon consisted of many acres of land sheltered by high, winding walls of rock, where the spring rains could gather on stony ground instead of sinking straight into the earth. The fertile soil left there by thousands of years of lush growth meant that it was alive with grass and trees, an oasis where settlers could make a living.

There was something odd about the canyon, the way it twisted into the ground. Cody could see straight away why it would have been a source of wonder to the people of the plains. The Chiricahuas wouldn't have settled here, any more than they would have settled anywhere else, but this fertile spot would have been a place where they could come and replenish their food stocks, and hunt bears.

No one could have said why, but there was an air of strangeness about the place. Cody broke the spell.

'Let's go down. Take your time, there's a lotta loose rock.'

9

'How in the name of St Patrick could such a thing be?' asked Donald.

'Easy,' said Jean. 'Jake explained it all to me. Seems like millions of years ago this place was what they call geologically active. What you're looking at is the result of volcanoes shooting up rock from way below the earth, then erosion from ice, wind, sun and water.'

'Never mind all that,' cut in Donald, 'let's get in there. I'll be glad to get out of the sun.'

'You're not going anywhere yet,' said Cody.

'Look, it's time for us to look for shelter,' said Jean. 'Once we're in we can ask the settlers for help.'

'You don't know who, or what is in there,' said Cody. 'I'm not trailing all this way to see you get killed.' He looked at the other men, who had come

149

just for treasure. 'Are you willing to explore a little?' The two merchants looked as if they would rather be elsewhere. Neither of them really wanted to face a potential danger. 'Of course, if you would rather wait here while I did the exploration, I would understand.'

''Course we are,' grunted Jackson.

'I'm up for it,' said Clemens.

They both looked as if they were biting down on a particularly sour piece of old meat. Pye merely looked ready to go.

'I'm coming too,' said Mary.

'Your father doesn't look all that well to me,' said Cody, shrewdly applying some pressure to the girl by other means than shouting or arguing. 'He needs you to look after him.'

Indeed he was correct in his assessment. Donald looked over-warm. He had visibly lost weight in just two days and he looked as if he was ready to get off his horse and lie down. Jean, too, was showing signs of wear. Normally a naturally chatty and vivacious woman, the death of her husband and the hot journey had worn her to a point where her temper could easily boil over.

'Mary, stay with your father. Let them go! They could be right. We don't know what's in there.'

Mary finally agreed to stay, but the look of rebellion on her fine features showed that next time she would not be so easily quelled.

Cody made sure that the wagon and the people were led to a sheltered spot. Mary and her father dismounted. She fetched some water from the wagon and made sure that he drank deeply, before getting him to lie down for a rest. Cody had been right, it was her fault that her parent was here in the first place. It was her duty to look after him. Her look of conciliation towards the young rider was wasted: he was riding onwards with the other three by then.

The whole party had descended from a height to a lower point. Now the four men could see that the path to the canyon was on an upward slope. Cody took the lead, the other three men letting him do so. Even though his weariness showed in every line of his body he kept himself rigidly upright and did not sway.

'As soon as we're out of sight, we can do what we started out to do,' said Jackson when they were far enough away from Donald, the two women and Cody himself, so that they could not be overheard.

'Not a good idea,' said Pye. 'The pup has some good reasoning. We don't know what's been happening. I doubt if there's an ambush waiting for us — the gang just ain't big enough — but there might be traps. What if the settlers themselves have been bought over? Just you two bide your time. We've come this far and it gets dark real soon.'

They soon found themselves riding into what could only be called an oasis in the midst of the desert, an oasis so big it was capable of supporting dozens, although not hundreds of people.

Sheltered from the desert, and descending a little into the fertile earth, fields of maize, potatoes, kale and other vegetables had been cultivated at the very start of the canyon where they would be watered by the fast-flowing monsoon rains, yet sheltered enough to be protected from the full force of the water that gave them nourishment.

Deeper inside the canyon itself, sheltered by more deep-red rocky walls, were the settlements of those who lived here. From the number of buildings that Cody counted as they rode along the dusty path in front of them, something like ten families had braved the desert to come and settle here.

Life here must be strange, he concluded, as he looked at these stone buildings. For a start the work would never end. The basics that others took for granted, even in a fairly unsophisticated place like Coker Town, were unavailable. If they wanted supplies they would have to travel many miles to the nearest town or city, relying on barter rather than money for what they could get.

These were not houses in the traditional sense. They had been manufactured from chunks of the local rock roughly hewn and fitted together. The roofs of the houses were made of timber that had been latticed together with ropes and then woven through with other plant materials. This construction method, speaking of the ingenuity of those who had made this little community, meant that these dwellings fitted in well with their natural surroundings. None of the buildings was fenced off from the others. Glass windows were rare, and extremely small.

Not a sound could be heard except for the faint clop of the horse's hoofs on the rocky ground. There was not even the bark of a dog, even though most people would have owned one in these circumstances. Cody could understand why this might be happening. Those who had moved to this area would not be used to having visitors, might already have had a run-in with the Mosse gang. Naturally they would be cautious about engaging with four armed men on horses coming into their simple farming community. He halted at the largest of the buildings that might belong to a community leader, and got off his horse.

'I'm going in,' he said to the other three. 'Cover my back.'

None of the rest would even have dreamed of shooting him by now. They needed the young man to do their dirty work and they were willing to let him go first. For obvious reasons Cody was speaking in almost a whisper. He went up to the building and stood, listening for any sounds behind the door. There was nothing except for the buzzing of flies and other insects. He did not hesitate after that, but pushed the door open and went inside.

His eyes took a moment to adjust to his surroundings as the light filtered in through the small window. Then he gasped in horror and shock at what he saw. A man of about his own age was lying on the ground. His throat had been cut so badly that his head was almost severed from his body. A woman lay across the room propped up on a wooden chair. Her garments had been half-torn from her body, one hand was held up as if in supplication and he saw that some of her fingers had been chopped off. Her legs were splayed open and it was obvious that whoever had killed her had taken her before completing the act. Or perhaps more than one of them had been using her. Her throat was cut too, the front of her simple country dress soaked stiff with her lifeblood. Flies were buzzing around the room and the stench of rotting meat made Cody realize that the people had been dead for quite a while — days at least. He knew that Jean had been admitting a simple truth when she kept Jake's body in a dark cellar, that people had to be buried quickly in the heat of Arizona. The flies were beginning to bother him now, attracted by the scent of fresh sweat from his long ride. He brushed them away but they just kept coming. He wanted to cry out in fear and annoyance and pure horror at the sight before his eyes and the insects attacking him so lustily, but for a second he was caught by the blonde hair of the woman, all that survived of her beauty, as it glinted faintly in the light that filtered through from the outside. He shook himself, waved the flies aside and half-stumbled to the entrance.

He came out of the building and walked down towards the three men. Pye was standing beside his horse.

'What's the matter, boy? You look as if you've seen a ghost.'

Cody said nothing. The buildings were well spaced apart. He took off and made a path across the brush to the next one, entering without even listening. If anything, this was worse than the last, a woman had been thrown against the wall where she lay propped at an awkward angle. It was obvious how she must have died because she had a gaping hole square in the middle of her chest. Worse still, two young children lay nearby, their throats cut so severely that they too had nearly had their heads severed. The sight of the two young corpses was enough for Cody. He staggered out of the building and stood against the outside wall, taking in a lungful of fresh air. The wound on his forehead, mending though it was, still throbbed and he could feel a faintness that threatened to engulf him.

He knew that a real man wasn't supposed to weep, but when he thought of what had been done to innocent children he felt a welling behind his eyes. In his mind, some of the fog that had bothered him for so long cleared. He was now cold and decisive regarding one fact: he was going to track down the gang and make them pay for what they had done.

Pye had gone into the original

dwelling. Now he came out and walked towards Cody, who still stood at the entrance to the next dwelling. The rider shook his head.

'Don't go in there, man.'

'As bad, is it?'

'Young 'uns this time. Murdered. Throats gashed. Their mother violated.'

'You really are in shock, Cody. Your face is whiter than any sheet I've slept on, your mouth is an almost invisible line.' It was the first time Pye had not used his name in a mocking manner. 'Guess you don't know anythin' about this?'

'If I had I wouldn't have come here with you.'

By this time the other two had dismounted. They came over to Pye.

'What is it?' asked Bud Clemens.

'Looks as if they've all been murdered,' said Pye grimly. 'Leastways they're dead in these here houses. You're welcome to check the rest soon as you like. I ain't doing it, I can tell you.'

'I won't bother,' said Clemens, suddenly shivering despite the warmth of the air around them.

'The bastards,' said Jackson. 'They murdered in cold blood.'

'You were going to do the same thing to me,' said Cody, his eyes widening as he stared at the saloon owner. Jackson put his hand down to his gun.

'You want to join them dead 'uns right now?'

Clemens was a little more circumspect.

'Ain't no good bringing up the past. We're here an' we've got to deal with this. I say we deal with it by getting the hell out and fergettin' this place ever existed.'

'Cut and run?' sneered Jackson. 'I ain't lighting out until I get some kind of profit for this one.'

Cody and Pye proved that they both had a great deal more tactical sense than the temporary deputies.

'Let's get the horses out of here,' said Pye, 'then we'll go further on foot, so nobody can hear us coming.' They led the horses around the curve at the mouth of the canyon. Cody now noticed that in the fields themselves hand tools for digging and cropping had been dropped as if those using them had fled at the sign of trouble. He cursed himself for not noticing this on the way in.

They went back into the canyon on foot. Neither of the deputies looked as if they wanted to be here. They all kept to the curving rocky walls of the settlement as they went, so that they would be a much smaller target, and skirted around the grim dwelling houses as they did so, none of them speaking as they looked for the prospective enemy.

They could see themselves that the territory they were in was shaped like a gigantic spiral; wide on the outside and narrowing like the shell of a snail to an inward point. When they looked up they could see natural ledges above them made of the same red, jagged rock, sometimes fringed with wild plants and bushes. It was from this point that the attack came.

They heard the sharp crack of a bullet ringing through the place they had reached together. It was an area of the canyon that had widened out, with large boulders strewn across the sandy ground interspersed with more sagebrush and long grass, which provided them with plenty of cover.

Cody glimpsed the figure of what could only be one of the outlaws above them on one of the rocky ledges. He was scrawny, his clothes as dusty as theirs.

As soon as he heard the gunfire, Pye ducked down out of sight along with Cody. The two men were taking the lead, with Cody just a little way ahead. They did not stay still in the undergrowth, for that meant that whoever was aiming at them would simply shoot into the same area until they were hit.

The gunman fired again, This time a bullet whizzed past Cody's right ear.

'I don't aim to get my ears pierced,' he said, whispering to Pye, showing that he was not without a sense of humour. 'You draw his fire and I'll get over to them rocks and shut him down.'

In the event Pye did not have to do anything. Jackson, who did not have the best of tempers, turned an interesting shade of puce when he discovered they were being shot at.

'The hell with this,' he said in his normal voice. With a boldness that belied his abilities, he ran out into the middle of the dip in the ground, pulled out his Colt and aimed at the figure up on the ledge. He did not even have a chance. The pistol gave another sharp crack and this time the saloonkeeper was wounded not in the leg, but in the chest. The gunman was reasonably close, so the powerful bullet passed through Jackson as if he was made of cobwebs, punching a bigger hole on the way out. As his blood spurted from him Jackson looked stupidly down at his chest and dropped his own gun, which fell to the ground with an audible thud. He may have been trying to speak, but his lungs had collapsed instantly when the bullet exited from his body, so that he gave only a wordless gurgle before collapsing on to his front.

In one way his intervention was lucky for Cody. While the gunman was dealing with his companion, the young rider ran into a position behind a large boulder on the other side of the path where he ducked down for a second, before rising and taking a potshot at the new foe.

The young man was both a good shot as well as being lucky. He hit the other gunman on the side of the right shoulder, the bullet taking out the gun hand so that he could not fire at them any more. The man, realizing that it was all over for him, tried to go backwards and get through whatever gap there was that led to his high vantage point but Cody immediately fired at him again. The gunman clutched at his side, gave a loud groan, and then staggered on what turned out to be a fairly narrow ledge. He missed his footing, gave a final yowl of fear and rage, and then crashed to the rocks below, his body landing with an audible crunch.

Pye and Clemens came from where they had been hiding then looked at the dead attacker and the body of Jackson Taylor. Bud Clemens was white, not with rage, but with fear. It was clear that he no longer wanted anything to do with this search for money, not if this was what it led to.

'We've got to get them bodies hidden,' said Cody. 'You two goin' to stand there like lemons, or you goin' to give me a hand?'

'What if the rest heard his attack on us?' asked Pye. 'He was a lookout after all.'

'Don't think they would've heard much,' said Cody. 'These walls are open to the sky, an' there's still a lot of growth as they go inwards. I think any noise we made was pretty localized. Trouble is, that must be a vulnerable point, which is why it was guarded. If we leave the bodies lyin' in plain sight that'll alert the first o' those bush-whackers who comes this way.'

Pye no longer argued with Cody, but conceded the point. Together, with the help of the ashen-faced Clemens, they worked to conceal the bodies. Because this was a wide area of the canyon, it had plenty of rocky rills and dips in the ground. They pulled the dead men into one of these hollows with a natural rocky projection above, pushing them in so that the dead were practically embracing in that narrow space. Pye, ever practical, had already garnered their weaponry. Then the three of them gathered a selection of boulders and smaller rocks, which they pushed in front of the makeshift burial spot. Cody then kicked dust over any signs of gore on the path. In just a few minutes it was as if the two men had never been.

For a second Cody wondered what it would be like in a hundred years when someone found them, when their story would be a mystery, and what theories those who discovered them would come up with.

The three travellers did not say a word to each other as they went back on to the path and retraced their steps. They fetched their horses which were peacefully grazing at the entrance and rode down to the others who were still sheltering at the wagon. Donald looked a lot more comfortable since resting and was in good spirits as he greeted their arrival.

'Hello, my friends! You're just in time for coffee, still bubbling I think.' Then his face fell as he noticed that one of them was missing. 'What happened?' he asked, standing looking up at them where they had halted. The two women came out from the other side of the wagon where they had been cooking in the shade.

'Is it Cody?' asked Mary anxiously as she came round. 'You're all right,' she said. The look on her face should have gladdened his heart, but his mind was so full of what had happened that he hardly noticed.

Bud Clemens got off his mount so hastily that he almost fell on his face. He half-staggered towards Donald and the two women.

'It was horrible; those people. That gunfight.'

'Cody might be all right,' said Pye, 'but Jackson ain't.' Briefly he related the story of their grim find. How a couple of dozen settlers at least were dead, then he went into their fight with the lookout man deeper in the canyon.

Everyone was shocked regarding what had happened to the people who had come here to live and work, just wanting to make a life for themselves in a green part of what could be an arid and inhospitable country. There was a real air of anger in the air against the Mosse gang. Looking for gold was all very well, but what they had done for that gold went against every code in the West, even that of outlaws. There could be no mercy for them now.

'Those poor people,' said Mary, 'we have to get in there and bury them.'

'You're not listenin',' said Pye. 'If any of us go back in there, the chances are we won't be comin' back out again.'

'They got to the place,' said Cody, 'but they had a couple of days on us, which makes me wonder why they're still here.'

'There might be a reason for that,' said Jean.

'What do you mean?'

'Well, you said that you had seen smoke the day before the Indians attacked us. Maybe the natives were further over towards Bear Canyon when the Mosse gang arrived and they waited out their time in a cave somewhere until they too saw the smoke signals further south.'

'You know, Jean, that's a mighty fine head you got on your shoulders,' said Pye. 'Pretty too.'

'Get away with you, Sheriff. There's also another reason why they've been delayed if that's the case.' Jean went

into the wagon and fetched the map.
'No use hiding this now from any of
you people.'

'Wait a minute.' Donald looked
beside himself with fury. 'That's what
it's been about all the time? Some story
about a hidden treasure? All those
people dead . . . you lot have rocks in
your head.'

'Look here,' said Jean, tracing the
charcoal lines with her finger. She had
traced Jake's map on to finely grained
buckskin rather than parchment. The
buckskin took the charcoal well and
when it was rolled up it was much less
susceptible to wind, heat and water
damage than even the best of paper.
'Jake hid his bounty at the base of a
rocky wall deep in the canyon, hard by
a silver birch — look, he even had those
words on the map.'

'So what?' asked Cody. 'That just
means they must have got in there,
found the landmark and dug out the
gold.'

'No, Jake seemed to *know* they were

after him,' said Jean. 'He didn't seem that surprised when they turned up at our homestead. Perhaps he had made the map as his own guide originally, but put a false marker in there in case it got stolen.'

'You mean the pine tree is a clue, but the place it's at isn't actually the location of the gold?'

'That's right, Cody.'

He studied the map for what seemed a long time, burning every single detail into his brain, as if it would be of great use in the near future. Jean held on to the leather as if she feared he might snatch it from her. Finally he gave her a slight nod and she rolled up the map and disappeared into the wagon to put it back into a secret hiding place only she knew.

Pye and Clemens looked at each other. It was obvious to Cody that they had not given up some of their ambitions in one area at least.

'Is that food I smell?' asked Pye heartily. 'Any to spare? A man can get hungry with all this work.'

The three men came to the small camp to get some food and hot coffee, but kept alert in case their altercation with the gunman had been heard. They did not take long to eat. Cody checked his guns were fully loaded and free of dust.

'Well, it's obvious that they're goin' to notice a man is missing,' he said, as he finished doing this. 'Now I suggest the rest of you get out of here.'

'What are you going to do?' asked Mary.

'I'm goin' to kill Kane,' said Cody, with a cool determination he could feel in every bone in his body.

10

'Sam, you can't let him go in there alone,' said Jean.

'It's his choice, m'dear.' Sheriff Pye simply shrugged his shoulders. 'Besides, I have something to say on the matter. Cody killed another man not two hours ago. Now, he was rightly defendin' Bud and me here. He's just announced he's goin' to find a man and kill him in cold blood. That's an offence any way you look at it.'

'Yeah, what do we really know about him?' sneered Clemens. 'Maybe he's always been a member of the gang really.'

'That I don't believe, not now,' said Pye. 'Upshot is, I say we let the young feller go in and find out what's doin'.'

'What do you mean?' asked Mary.

'If we don't see him doin' anythin'

wrong to the gang there's nothin' we can do with regards to the law, especially if they're not around to say what happened. As for sayin' I can't arrest him, you're wrong there: I was asked to uphold the law in the territory and there's not a court in the land would say I hadn't acted proper in bringin' him in — if he does wrong.'

Donald looked as if he wanted to tear his hair out.

'Listen, we can take some of the crops belonging to those poor people, water from the well, and just plain get out of here.'

'We can't do that, sir,' said Cody, his jaw set in a square, determined line. 'Not after what I saw.'

'Those poor people,' said Mary. 'We have to be sensible and wait for this thing with the gang to be cleared out of the way, but we have to bury them. We can't leave them like that.' She grasped Cody by the arm. 'If you go in just now, do you promise to have a look-see and come straight back?'

'The girl shows some tactical sense,' said Pye.

'Mary' — Donald looked at his daughter — 'just think of what this is going to do to your mother if either of us gets harmed or killed.'

She looked at her father, eyes filled with tears, but it was obvious that she was one with a stubborn heart. 'Daddy, I'm sorry, but we're in this now. We can't get away without their help and I know that you'll do everything to protect me.'

'All I want to do,' put in Jean, 'is to get the gold that belonged to myself and Jake, go back home and lead a peaceful life. It's really not that much to ask for. But, Cody, you've shown yourself to be a good, resourceful man, please don't go in there guns blazing and get yourself killed to no purpose.' There was a gleam in her eye when she said this. He was facing a very different Jean from the one he had met at the Slash T. For a start she had twisted her long blonde hair back and tied it into a ponytail. She had donned a plain black dress and her speech had hardened. She was not the soft, distressed woman he had first encountered. He had the feeling that perhaps she was asking him not to get killed for her sake rather than his. This was confirmed with her next words. 'If you alert them to the fact we're here they won't leave a single one of us unharmed, so go, but for our sakes and the money involved, be careful.'

'This hasn't even started yet,' said Cody. 'All of us are involved in this. It's obvious these men don't play around. We got to set things up so we have the maximum advantage. For a start we have to get the wagon out of here.' He looked around at the rocky landscape. The faint trail that had been used by the settlers when leaving this isolated place snaked along and beside the nearest mesa. They had been taking the path of least resistance. 'Take the wagon and go down there,' he said, pointing to the mesa. 'It'll automatically put you in shadow and keep you both away from any fighting that might occur.' He was speaking directly to the two women now. 'Then at least you'll have a chance because they won't know you're there.' He looked at the two older men. 'You'll have to be mounted and wait with loaded guns at the rim of the canyon just in case I have to run and they're comin' after me. Truth is, that's unlikely to happen, if there's a ruckus chances are I'll be dead long before I can get even close to you, but if they come looking for anyone you'll be in a position to shoot 'em dead. Donald, you'll be on a high point within firing range, but hidden, where you can take potshots at 'em.'

Bud Clemens looked rather like a fat squirrel that had bit down on a sour pickle. He was not taking lightly to being ordered about by a possible miscreant who, just a couple of days ago, they had been trying to hang. Pye, however, looked as if he was rather enjoying himself.

'I could see there was spirit in you,' he said. 'Now you're showin' a lotta tactical sense.'

'We need less talk and more action,' said Cody. 'Well, ladies, no time like the present. Before I do anything we stock up on water and some of the settlers' provisions.' This took them about an hour. Donald worked enthusiastically to help them achieve this aim. At least it looked as if his daughter was going to be safe.

Jean, too, looked rather astounded at the change in the young man who had grown so much in confidence from the time when she had seen him ensconced in a prison cell. She hitched up her horses and the wagon was swiftly drawn to the spot he had pointed out a quarter-mile away.

'It's time now,' said Cody.

'Wait!' cried Mary, as he started to go.

'What?'

'Bend down from your saddle, I have something to say.'

He did as he was asked and was astonished when she kissed him full on the lips. He felt a different stirring from that of the anger that had been in him ever since the grim discovery in Bear Canyon.

'There's more of that when you come back, so promise you will.'

He was speechless, but nodded at her then rode off at a steady pace. The big black stallion was no longer as skittish as he had once been. It was as if he had a sense of what was going on. The other men had already taken up position outside the canyon as he rode through the entrance. He went past the settlement that had now become a tomb for those who had thought they were starting out on a new life, then down towards the inner part of the huge canyon. Finally he dismounted and tied his horse to a tall bush. He whispered something in Satan's ears and the horse flattened his ears back and appeared to listen earnestly. Cody patted his neck, then set off on foot.

He was just beside the ledge from which the wounded man had plunged to his doom not that long ago. How had he gotten up there? Cody went onwards and saw that there was an almost regular corridor of rock that sloped steadily downwards until it came out at a wooded pass that must lead to the very centre of Bear Canyon. No wonder no one had heard their shots, the shape of the place and the trees must have acted as a natural baffle, channelling the sounds upwards and away from this spot.

Cody did not go down to the pass itself. There was no point in doing so. If indeed it was where the gang were hidden it would be like going straight into a nest full of sidewinders which would strike with venom.

He retraced his steps. The rocky walls were not straight, but sloped upwards from the broken ground. One split in the walls resembled a trail of sorts, a broken trail littered with stones, but one which acted as a natural stairway that a man could climb if he was careful and took his time. Cody decided that he had the time; since there was no other way he could go. He made sure that his guns were firmly holstered since it wouldn't do to lose either of them when going into such a potentially dangerous situation, then he pushed himself up the slope. Soon he discovered it really was like climbing a steep flight of stairs. Each time he moved upwards he got a little higher, but if he stopped at particular parts of the slope he began to slide down again. It reminded him of the game of Snakes and Ladders.

Despite this he was able to make good time and soon the slope turned into a natural plateau, with some greenery. As he rested his aching legs he looked over and saw he was on the wooded ledge where the man had been guarding the entrance. Satan was just below. He went over to where the man had rested, and found amongst other things a bedroll, some dried food and water, along with the remains of a campfire over which the man had boiled his water and cooked his food.

That was when he heard the sound of the footsteps below.

★ ★ ★

Mary hid in the shadows for approximately ten minutes before she began to chafe at the restriction imposed for her own safety.

'This isn't any good,' she told Jean. 'We're skulking about here when we could be helping Cody. Pye just wants to see him dead, that's why he sent them in there.'

'I don't think so, young lady,' said Jean. 'That wouldn't be in his own interests.'

'Yes it would, I've been thinking about it. What Pye does is, he sends in Cody. Cody is not the subtlest of men, he attracts the attention of the gang and they pursue him towards the entrance, then Pye and the other two ambush them and kill or wound them.'

'That would mean a lot of risk for Pye.'

'You know the sheriff is a brave man. He's also a superb shot. If he waits at the entrance, chances are he'll be able to pick off most of them with Dad and Clemens to back him up. In the meantime, Cody gets caught in the middle and I can guess what his chances are.'

'Well, there's nothing we can do.'

'Have you any weapons?'

'Yes.' Jean took a quick inventory. 'I have a couple of pistols and about thirty rounds of ammunition.'

'Let's get in there and back Cody up. Or at least give the impression that's what we're going to do.'

A few minutes later they were at the top of the slope. Donald saw them coming and came out from behind his shelter of boulders to wave them away.

'Go back!' he called.

His daughter waved to him, then she faced up to the sheriff.

'This isn't any good. You've got to go in there and help him.'

'See, that wasn't the plan,' he said. 'Doesn't make sense. This way we can catch 'em like rabbits in a trap.'

'Really? And what if Cody really is a member of the gang? What if he managed to fool us all the whole time?'

'I don't think he is.'

'Can you take that chance? You saw yourself what they did to those settlers.'

'We'll take our chances,' said Pye, so complacently that the girl turned red with fury.

'Well, I'm going in.'

'No, you're not,' said Donald, who had arrived by this time. 'I'll tie you up first, my girl.'

'Perhaps she's right,' said Pye, 'maybe we could just keep an eye on this maverick. You up for it, Donald?'

'Only if you promise to keep out of it,' said Donald to his daughter. 'You too, Jean. I would have thought you would have been more sensible than to let her come up here.'

'I ain't coming with you,' said Bud Clemens, white with fear.

'That's OK, Bud, stay with the girls,' said Pye, his voice full of contempt. 'You coming, Donald?'

'Yep.' Together the men rode down towards what might be an all-or-nothing situation.

It was better than just waiting.

* * *

The footsteps halted below the plateau. Cody had to act quickly. He could take the man out. It was unlikely the rest at this distance would hear his shots, but then the arrival, whoever he was, would be missed quickly depending on what was happening in the centre of the area.

'Yay, Parsons, it's McCourt. You still there, you lazy sheep-worrier?'

Luckily the ledge was covered with bushes that grew tall to reach light from the sun. Cody stood in such a way that his shape could be seen faintly through the undergrowth but could still make him largely invisible to the man below.

'Yep, OK,' he said, lowering and roughening his voice at the same time.

McCourt, a big man with a bull neck and a sloping forehead indicating that he was perhaps not the most intelligent member of the gang, was also tired, hot and dusty and a little resentful at having to walk up here.

'OK, ya can come back down now. We're nearly finished down there. 'Nother coupla hours an' we ride out. Ya seen anyone?'

'Naw.'

'Won't wait for ya. Takes a bit to get down here. Gotta go.' The man turned round and tramped off. Cody pulled back from the ledge. He had learned a lesson: it was better to confront on your own terms. He could easily have killed the bull-necked gang member, but that would have led to all sorts of complications that might had led to his, Cody's, demise.

He discovered that he was trembling, not from fear, but rather from the desire to get in there and destroy those who had tried to destroy him. Once more, when he was up there he had to control his desires or he might well wreck his own plans.

Turning away from his spot overlooking the pass once the other man had retreated into the distance, Cody climbed upwards on the broken trail. It was not an easy climb and required determination. One slip and the person making their way up would find themselves sliding rapidly down a steep slope with sharp rocks on either side ready to tear them to ribbons.

Finally he got to the top and found himself on a mountainous area with jagged rocks on one side and a slope that led down towards the pass on the other, but still hard for a man to climb. The area was covered in low bushes, spiky grass and withered-looking trees much more starved of water than those down below yet still managing to retain a foothold in the rocky soil.

Cody had a good bump of direction.

He went towards the pass, but moving as slowly as he could. He could not know that by this time Donald and Pye were on his trail. Up here he felt totally alone and in a different world. What made it worse was the fact that as he came closer to the edge, he had to walk more slowly so that he did not rattle loose stones over the rim, alerting the gang to his presence. As he moved he looked to his left. There, on the very edge of the slope, was a gigantic boulder that had come to rest here eons ago and now sat on the edge of the gap that led to the wooded valley where the Mosse gang were hiding.

Cody knew, somehow, that he had seen such things before. These boulders often sat like this, balancing on a knife-edge until monsoon floods swept them downwards again. This one was sitting atop a pile of loose earth and rock. Shifting the boulder would unleash an avalanche of huge proportions and would seal the gap even better, preventing the gang from rolling the boulder to one side. He doubted very much if they had dynamite with them, and a sudden hope surged through his breast. He looked around for something he could use as a lever. He didn't have to look far. Many of the trees had been riven by the spring storms and the mountain was littered with branches. He picked up one of these. It was dry, about four feet long, and felt rough to the touch. The tip of the branch had a rough arrow shape where it had broken from the tree. If he put this to the base of the huge boulder and applied leverage, Cody knew that he would stand a good chance of sealing the gang inside the valley.

First he made his way to the edge and, with great caution, looked over. The remaining five members of the Mosse gang were finishing loading the wagon with bars of gold. Bullion! Cody, in his wisdom, had pictured the gold as raw nuggets, but these were bars that were shaped into the traditional oblong shape. From this distance he could not see the stamp on them, but he was sure it would be from a federal bank.

From where he lay he could see that various parts of the rocky surface had been breached, with half-a-dozen partial excavations visible. He could only imagine what effort had been spent here looking for the treasure of Jake Thatcher.

There in the middle of the valley, leaning against the silver birch outlined on the map, was the figure of Kane smoking a cigarette. He was indeed a tall, rangy man, with a trace of face fungus. Cody understood immediately why Jean, in the semi-darkness of the sheriff's office, had mistaken him for Cody. They had roughly the same build, even though even at this distance, Kane was clearly an older man.

'Finished loading,' said McCourt, who had obviously set to work immediately on his arrival back at the site.

'OK. Where's Parsons, thought you went to tell him the good news?' asked Kane.

'He said he was on his way,' grunted McCourt. 'Bet you a dollar he's waitin' for us to come out an' get him.'

'Well, he ain't gettin' as big a share,' said Kane. He grinned wolfishly. 'Boys, it took us a long time to work out that cuss Jake Thatcher had lied on his map as to where the gold was concealed, but we did it.'

'No, you did,' said McCourt. 'You worked out it was in a cave marked by the noonday shadow of this here tree.'

'Get them horses fixed to the wagon,' said Kane, who did not seem to want to wallow in his final triumph, perhaps because it could also have been pointed out that they had made many false starts before correctly reading the clues on the map. 'Time we got rollin'.'

Cody moved back and froze as some loose scree — a mixture of tiny stones and soil — rattled down the side of the cliff.

One of the men cursed aloud.

'What was it?' he said. 'Think someone's after us?'

'Just some loose stuff,' said Kane, 'it's rattled down before but we was too busy diggin' to notice. Get those horses, I said.'

Cody hardly trusted himself to sigh in relief. He pulled back even further and inched towards the huge rock. The branch was still lying where he had left it. He was by no means sure that he could get it to shift, even with a lever, but he was going to try.

There was no other choice.

11

Donald and Sam Pye found Satan and left their horses beside him. They reckoned what was good enough for Cody would do for them. They walked along the fresh trail he had left, but cautiously, guns drawn. If Cody had already been captured then their lives were already in danger.

Pye had already been there and he, too, had worked out that if there had been a sentry there must be some way of getting up to him. Further along, it was he who pointed out the break in the rock face that formed a natural stairway up to where the man had been hidden.

'This is where we're goin',' announced the sheriff. Donald looked at the gap and groaned aloud.

'We're not built for this.'

'The hell with it,' said Pye. 'Least-ways we won't be waitin' for lightning to fall on us this way.'

Donald went first. Luckily all his hard work in the hardware store had left him with some trace of the sinews he had in his youth. By dint of rushing up the first slope and grasping either side then resting he was able to make good progress. Pye took much longer and his face went an interesting shade of puce, which meant he was paying for all those free dinners in Jackson's saloon.

They were both nearly at the ledge — with Donald giving the lawman a helping hand to get there — when they heard an almighty rumble from the other side of the rill. There was a grumble like a giant roaring in his sleep, then a series of crashes followed by a shock wave that nearly tumbled them back down to where they had come from.

'Earthquake!' shouted Donald.

'No, avalanche,' said Pye. 'Heard this type o' thing before.'

They both waited until the shock

waves subsided, then had to decide
what to do.

* * *

Cody, when he set off the avalanche,
really had no idea what he was letting
himself in for. He put the branch
beneath the giant boulder, shoved hard,
and, as he felt it rock, his boots slipped
against the loose ground. For a moment
he nearly fell. When he regained his
balance the giant boulder had not
shifted at all. Chagrined, he tried again.
It rocked against the ground, but did
nothing else. He was not wearing gloves
and the rough branch was digging into
his hands, lacerating the skin, and
making them bleed. He could hear the
clop of hoofs now as the horses in the
valley began to move. He also heard
shouts.

'There *is* some critter up there,
Kane.'

'Yay, I think so. Come on, boys, let's
get outa here.'

'What about the ass up there?'

'Just go.'

In another second his plans would be destroyed and he would have to try and get back to Satan then fight five angry outlaws. The outcome looked bleak.

Cody took a deep breath even though the wound on his forehead throbbed deeply. Some memory came back to him that if he applied a force steadily, it would work far better than just attacking the rock. He applied the lever below, concentrating on this one task, shutting out the raised voices, the sound of the horses, the rumble of the wagon laden with gold bullion. All that existed was Cody and the rock. This time he applied a smooth pressure, and this rocked the boulder. As it came back he applied the same pressure again. This time it rocked a little more. The third time he was able to see a widening gap beneath the boulder. He shoved the lever into this and gave a last heave and the boulder began to roar down the slope.

With the reactive senses of one who was young, Cody now realized that he was in terrible danger. The loose rocks and stones beneath him began to act more like water than hard material and began to flow downwards towards the pass like their giant companion. Luckily he was able to grasp on to a low bush. He pulled himself to safety and scrambled as fast as he could away from the avalanche, higher up the cliff and found a place where the ground was steady. The noise and dust were tremendous, and he tied his spotted red bandanna around his lower face and pulled his hat down low so that he was not blinded or choked by the dust. The noise was so loud he thought his eardrums were going to burst.

As the avalanche subsided he could hear the frightened horses whinnying below and the curses of the men as they tried to keep them under control.

Even more cautiously than before, Cody edged towards the rim of the cliff and peered over. The men were too busy concentrating on what they were doing to bother with him, except for one.

Kane looked up and saw the young rider looking down at them. He was gloved, ready to ride. He also had the look of a man who was ready to kill on the slightest pretext. Cody was pleased at the thought that at least they were separated. But he was wrong. Kane looked at the side of the valley, the projecting rocks and sturdy bushes that grew out of the wall, and he began to climb. He only had fifty feet or so to cover, and he moved with the agility of a mountain goat, finding both foot and handholds that would have defeated other men. As he climbed he screamed down at his gang, some of whom were looking at him as if he had taken leave of his senses.

'Cover me!'

The rising dust from the avalanche was also an immeasurable help to the furious killer in his rapid ascent. It was as if the valley was filled with a fine mist. When Cody looked over at the roiling, fog-like dust curling up from the rocks that had rained down from above like water, all he could catch was the odd glimpse of the man who was coming to get him.

Worse than that, even as Cody leaned over he heard a shout.

'Abe, can you see him?' the guttural tones of McCourt sounded out.

'He's over there,' said Abe, another member of the quintet.

Cody felt a hail of bullets zing past his ear like angry hornets. He pulled back rapidly. It seemed they could see him from their position better than he could glimpse them from his, which was fair enough since the sun was behind him while he was looking into a darker area. If they had not been there he would have been able to solve the problem of Kane quickly enough, but as it was he felt it was more than prudent to get away from the edge. He moved higher up the slope, safe in a new sense of superiority.

Of course! All he needed to do was wait until Kane appeared and shoot him off the edge. Cody felt no compunction about what he was about to do. Kane had been the instrument of a terrible wrong. He had wounded an innocent man and left him for dead. He had terrorized a woman, widowed her and threatened her with rape. Worst of all, he had authorized the murder and violation of peaceful settlers who had no quarrel with anyone. There could be no mercy whatsoever for such a person. Besides, he suspected that the territory would thank him for sending the leader of the notorious Mosse gang to hell. Such was Cody's confidence; he stood out in the open with his gun at the ready, just waiting to send Kane tumbling back down to oblivion.

What he had not taken the time to figure out was that Kane was an old campaigner who was not going to make a wooden soldier target to practise on. Instead, a hand came over the edge of the cliff and a shot rang out in Cody's direction, then a long, lean figure flung itself over the top and rolled behind the safety of a line of raised rocks. It was obvious that Kane had mapped out the area before going to dig for gold.

Cody uttered a loud curse as the bullet shattered some rock and raised splinters that went straight through his jeans and grazed the flesh of the leg. He ran as if he was on fire, sheltering behind a large bush that afforded little enough cover.

'Give up, Kane, you're finished,' he yelled. 'Your men are trapped an' there's a sheriff on your trail.'

The answer was a bullet that went straight through the bush and thudded uncomfortably close into the wall of rock behind him.

'You pissant,' yelled Kane. 'You're dead meat for what you've done!'

Feeling as if he was being suffocated, Cody tore off his bandanna. As he did so the motion knocked off his hat, but he felt a rush of air into his lungs. He jumped from behind the bush, both guns blazing at the same time. He was elated when he heard Kane give a loud groan. He had wounded his enemy. He caught a glimpse of a dark-clad figure rolling towards greater shelter — a clump of three mountain ash trees growing in one fertile patch of ground. Kane did not waste any time, leaping to his feet, aiming through a gap between the trunks and loosing off a hail of bullets. Cody jumped to one side, a bullet nicking just his left shoulder as he did so. A few inches lower it would have ripped a deep wound. Then, strangely, Kane's guns fell silent.

'Give yourself up and you might live,' snarled Cody.

'Cody, is that you?' Kane's voice suddenly sounded very different indeed.

'Who the hell are you, coming out with my name?' asked Cody. The wound on his forehead had healed considerably, but that faintness he had experienced before came over him at the sound of Kane's voice uttering his name. It was a familiar tone, much like his own, the inflection, everything. Cody had the overwhelming impression that he was on the brink of an important revelation.

'Cody, it's me, Kane.'

'I know you, Kane Mosse.' He steadied his guns. 'You'll surrender or die.'

'My name isn't Mosse, it's Banks, just like yours. Mosse is dead.'

'What kind of trick is this?' yelled Cody.

'No trick at all. Jordan Mosse formed the gang six years ago. He was gunned down durin' a raid on a rich merchant, but by then we was known as the Mosse Boys an' the name stuck.'

'What do you mean we share the same name, you bullcrap bastard?'

'Cody, you don't know me? I'm your brother.'

Cody suddenly felt as if the ground had been pulled from under him. His head was in a wild confusion, and for a moment he almost dropped his guns, then he leaned his back against the woody stem of the bush as a flood of memories came back to him so rapidly that at first he was unable to cope with them. He made himself breathe slowly and steadily.

'She sent me, that's right.' He passed a hand over his forehead. He felt that at any moment his head was going to burst.

'Who?'

'The woman who . . . ' The foggy memory suddenly become a face in his mind. 'Mom.'

'What about her? Ah'm comin' over there.'

'You do, you'll be dead.'

'Cody! Why did Mom send you?'

Cody spoke to his invisible enemy now, the enemy who was his brother, whom he still could not trust.

'She sent me to tell you Pa died a few months ago. She heard you was in trouble; a neighbour told us you had become one of the Mosse gang.' It was all flooding back to him now. Their ranch in the north, the day his mother had seen him away at the door, his idealism, the way he had been sure that he would be able to bring her eldest son back.

'She knew you'd been good to me when we was young, despite how you an' Pa quarrelled so bad with each other, an' she thought I could make you come back, be a rancher. I guess she was wrong.' He could not keep the bitterness out of his last few words.

'Pa's dead?' Kane sounded hoarse with anger. 'Good! He beat up on me so much I sometimes couldn't stand. If I hadn't left the old bastard would've been a goner a lot sooner. The only reason I hung around for so long was to protect Ma. When Pa got ill and you two had to run things, that's when it was time for me to go.'

Cody felt the faintness and weariness start to engulf him. Standing upright, he took in lungfuls of air. Now that the rock dust had started to clear he was able to do so without choking. The sensation did not entirely clear; neither did the fog still inside his head.

'Your gang attacked me, Kane. I didn't deserve that. I know it was them. You killed an innocent man too. I would have died if some good people hadn't rescued me.'

'What happened, Brother, was simple enough. You ran into us as we was making our way from the Thatcher spread. 'Stead of ridin' by and minding your own business you approached us. The boys were skittish — who can blame them, now that we finally knew where that toad had hidden our gold? They thought you was some kind of lawman.'

'Why would they think that?'

'Just that you had the bearing of a man on a mission. So I decided to take care of it. You had your hat pulled low on your face. It was only when you raised your head and I saw under the brim that I recognized who you were. Look, this is what clinched it for me.' There was a grunt as the wounded man threw something. His aim was good and the object fell through the under-growth and landed at Cody's feet. He picked it up without thinking. It was a bear's claw, the fur, leathery pad and claws carefully preserved, with a piece of rawhide string attached. Cody turned it over in his hands and felt yet another memory stir in his mind.

'That was the clincher for me. I knew you really was my brother when I saw that. You see, it was me gave it to you when you was a kid, just before I hit the trail so many years ago.'

'So you decided to kill me.'

'You really don't remember?'

'Don't you see the wound on my forehead?'

'I gave you that wound. I hit you so hard that you fell off your horse straight to the ground. I've been knocking people out for a long time and I figured I had hit you enough to lay you cold without permanent damage. Looks like I miscalculated a-ways. Told them you were dead. Sure looked that way at the time.'

'Why would you do that at all?'

'Because they woulda killed you right away.'

'You shot my horse too.'

'Wasn't me, it was one of the others. Parsons, I think. My hands were tied. If I'd told them not to do it they woulda known something was up, then they woulda turned on me too. When we rode off I took a look back. It was cooling down in the desert, you was going to wake.'

'I would have died, alone, from exposure.'

'It was evening. I knew that folks would be returning to Coker Town, I figured you would get picked up and helped.'

'And if I hadn't?'

'Cody, I did the bestest I could at the time. You don't understand these men. None of them is the slightest bit soft.'

'You hurt an innocent man. Not me, I don't care about that, not any more; you killed a man who just wanted to live a peaceful life.'

'That sidewinder was the worst of us,' said Kane. 'He hid the gold here an' left us to stew. Two of us went to Yuma under other charges — I was one of them. The others quarrelled and broke up with each other. That meant they didn't get it together to get Jake.'

'So you got out of prison?'

'Yep, two years in that hell-hole, just Parsons and me. He didn't have no brains to speak of; he just wanted to find Thatcher and blow a hole in him.'

'You thought different?' Despite himself Cody found that he was growing interested.

'Cody, I'm gettin' old when it comes to this stuff. The Mosse gang promised easy pickin's, but it never worked that way. The gold was the best thing that ever happened to us. This was to be the last ever, for all of us. We've got some dynamite in the wagons. Let me go. I'll get us out of here and we'll disappear, start new lives. You can tell Ma I'm a businessman. Look, I'll even cut you into the deal. That was the trouble with

Jake, he wanted it all for himself. If he'd been square with us he'd still be alive.'

For a moment Cody was sorely tempted. He could help his brother get the gold out of Bear Canyon, and he would never be poor again. The memories flooding back now spoke only of poverty and back-breaking work on a smallholding, not a life to which any sensible person would return. He certainly didn't owe anything to Clemens or Pye. He also knew that none of the party really had his best interests at heart: except for one person, that was . . .

There, in his mind he saw Mary. He knew that she would not approve if he went over to this outlaw life, that in fact he would lose her forever for a reason he had already encountered on their arrival at this benighted place. He discovered, to his surprise, that he did not want to relinquish the girl.

'Kane, I'm taking you in,' he said wearily. 'This cannot stand.'

'Why? Don't you see what you'll be missing?'

'Sure I do, but there's just one problem, Kane: I saw what you did to those settlers. Now, do you want a fight, or do you surrender now?'

12

While the two men rested on the rocky ledge just after the avalanche, they crouched in silence until the noise and shaking all but subsided. The impact on their side of the hill was so great at first that they were nearly knocked back down to where they had come from.

At the top of the broken trail there was a minor pass with scrub and stone on either side. Donald was the first to get to this point with the sheriff close behind him. They were still concealed from the wide top of the plain, but close enough to hear what was going on. That was when both of them heard the gunfire as Cody tried to shoot Kane off the face of the cliff, then the exchange of shots from those below. At last they heard the revelation that Kane was Cody's brother, and that the assault had been an attempt to save the young man's life in the face of savage, unprincipled men who would stop at nothing in their hunger for the precious metal.

Pye pushed Donald out of the way and moved forward slowly, holding a pistol in his hand, locating Kane by the sound of his voice. He knew that the outlaw would be a good shot just by having had to use his skills so much. If he were going to deal with him he, Pye, would have just one chance. It was the way of things.

★   ★   ★

'The settlers? What about them?'

'You somehow managed to slaughter every man jack of them. Probably arrived as thieves in the night, slaughtered little kids, mothers too, raped their women.' Cody could not keep the disgust and horror from his voice. 'For that alone you deserve to die. You're my brother; you might have saved me in the end, but nothing can forgive what you did to those people.'

'Cody, I swear to you, that wasn't us. What happened was, after we left Jake dead we went into Coker Town for supplies then rode out into the desert real quick. While we was in the town we heard a rumour that some Injuns had escaped from their reservation where they shoulda stayed good and proper.'

'But this was their land,' said Cody. 'Maybe they had some right to feel angry it was being taken from them.'

'Don't matter none, fact was we didn't want to tackle nobody, so we used our trackin' skills and saw that they was sendin' out their smoke signals from this very area. We didn't want a fight. We can battle with the best of them, but only when it's for our own gain and them Apaches don't mess around.'

'So what did you do?'

'We figured that if they was on the warpath they wouldn't be hanging around the one place for too long, so we just plain hid from them in one of the gullies that are so plentiful around here. They passed us real close at one point and we thought there would be a fight, but we outsmarted them in the end.'

Cody realized that the outlaws had not been as far from the party as they feared, that indeed they might have caught up with them if it had not been for the warring tribesmen.

'So we comes here and, like you, we thought we could get some help from the settlers. That was when we found every man jack of them was dead and the women violated. Just at that time we was outraged all right. We wished we had stayed there and fought them right enough, but by that time it was too late, so I just stayed in here and made the men dig. We had to get on with it because we didn't know when or if they were comin' back. That's why we had a lookout. If he scrambled over and warned us at least we would have a fightin' chance if the Injuns returned. His name was Parsons, I don't know where he went.'

'Those Indians regard this as a sacred place,' said Cody, 'to them this is where the sacred Bear lives. When they came across them settlers they regarded that in the same way we look on blasphemy. That's why they slaughtered them. It doesn't mean it's right what they did to the women or children, but you can understand their actions.'

'Nope, never could and never will,' said Kane.

'As for your man Parsons, he's dead. He attacked our party and I shot him down. He would have finished us otherwise.'

'Can't say I'm sorry. He wasn't the brains of the bunch, an' greedy too. He would've been trouble, that one, when it came to dividing up the goods.'

'As for the Indians, it doesn't make it right, but they attacked us not two days back and I got nearly a dozen of them.' Cody was not boasting about the matter, in fact there was sadness in his voice. A lot of people who wanted to make their life in this oasis had died, and a lot of young tribesmen had been slaughtered needlessly. That it was their own fault was not really the issue when you realized that their tribe had been badly wronged by the authorities. Injustice could create a lot of anger.

Now that Cody had discovered that his brother was not the murderer he had thought, he decided to take him in rather than gun him down.

'Kane, surrender and I'll make sure you get a fair trial.'

'I'll make you a better offer, Cody: again I say to ya, come with us and you'll get Parson's share of the goods.'

For a moment Cody was sorely tempted. He had lived a hard life. Those riches would enable him to have a life he could never obtain by hard work alone. But for Kane it was too late, he had chosen his path. Cody thought of his mother and Mary, and knew what his choice had to be.

'No. Now give up.' It was time for

action. He leapt from behind his shelter and zigzagged forward towards the dark figure lurking behind the boulders. There was a roar of thunder while a bare second later he felt a blazing hot pain in his fingers and the weapon went spinning from his hand. His fingers were still whole but even so it hurt like blazes. A second later, before he had time to recover and aim his second gun the dark figure leapt forward and brought down the butt of his weapon so hard on the other hand that Cody immediately dropped that one too. There was a clatter as Kane kicked it out of the way.

Cody fell back as Kane pushed him away and he felt a raw, bitter humiliation that he had been taken out so easily.

'Here, Brother, take this. I wish to hell you'da listened to some sense.' Kane stuffed the bear claw that had fallen from his brother's pocket down the front of Cody's shirt. 'If it wasn't for that you woulda died a while ago.

Now, thanks to you we've got men's work to do.'

He went to the edge of the cliff and looked down at his men.

'You sorted out, boys?' There was a faint reply as they shouted back to him. It seemed that were indeed 'sorted out'. 'All right. Get the dynamite and blast a hole in that thing. The rock's kinda loose so you should get a hole there easy. I'll join ya on the other side.' Kane was well aware that it would be a lot harder to climb down the steep face than it had been to get up. Especially now that he had a wounded shoulder which gave him the full use of only one arm.

Cody was young, and a lot more resilient than he looked on the outside. His hands, although still sore from the blows he had received, soon recovered their feeling, giving him the impetus for his next act. He surged forward and caught hold of Kane by the neck and pulled him away from the edge. His rage was enormous, but not great enough to let his brother take a fall that would almost certainly have led to mortal injury.

Kane staggered backwards and nearly fell, showing his mettle by ducking down and breaking his brother's grip, then turning to face him with a look that did not bode well for his younger sibling.

'I tried to reason with you, pup, looks as if I'm going to have to lay you out a lot worse than before.' Kane moved back, nearly tripping on the stones beneath his feet as he sought to draw his gun. He only had one weapon. Cody was not about to let this happen and surged forward again, knocking the man to the ground and straddling over him while he clawed at the holster. The gun went spinning across the uneven surface, out of their mutual reach.

With a grunt of pain, the older man pushed Cody off and managed to stagger to his feet. Kane punched his brother several times on the face, so hard that it would have knocked down a lesser man. They parted, snarling furiously at each other. The younger man bunched up his fists and punched Kane deliberately on his wounded shoulder. He just wanted to bring this to an end.

Kane shouted in pain, gave some ground and fell away from Cody. Then his hard eyes lighted on something on the ground behind his younger brother. It was the gun that had been taken from him when they were on the ground just seconds ago.

He dived forward, grabbed the weapon and got to his feet. If he had been in prime physical condition he would have gotten the drop on his brother quickly enough, but such was the force of his movements that he carried on across the rocks and had to force his body to turn. In the meantime, Cody saw that the gun was not pointing at him, so he took a split-second decision to wrest the weapon from Kane.

The two men wrestled on the very edge of the fifty-foot drop into the valley below. For a few seconds it seemed as if the two of them were going to go over the edge. Cody could feel the empty space at his side. He experienced the sickening feeling in the pit of his stomach that this was how it was going to end. Yet somehow they both pulled away from danger.

As Kane had only one fully functioning arm, Cody finally managed to grab the gun away from his brother's grip. Cody fell back, pointing the weapon straight at his brother's heart.

'That thing ain't loaded,' said Kane, panting hard. A thin trickle of blood came from his nostrils. He wiped this away with the back of his right hand.

'Well, you seemed to be mighty keen to get it on me,' said Cody. 'Get your hands up.'

'I ain't doing nothing you tell me, sonny.' Kane did not even bother trying to lift his arms.

'Kane, you'll see it's for the best.

You'll get sentenced, you'll serve some time, but you'll come out and the farm'll be yours.'

'You'd let me become a cropper? Mighty good of you, Brother.'

'Come on. We'll get you down off this place. I'll get the others to deal with your men.'

'You're throwing away an easy life.'

'No, I ain't. Sometimes the easy way's the hardest. If you had all the funds you wanted you'd be dead in less than a year from the fightin' an booze. Now get shifting.'

Kane looked behind Cody.

'Look out, Brother.'

'That's the oldest trick in the book,' said the young man, not even turning his head. There was the crack of a pistol, and then a red flower blossomed in Kane's chest over his heart. The gang leader staggered backwards, but did not say a word, his dark eyes levelled on Cody. Then Kane vanished as he fell off the cliff, dead long before he hit the ground.

'No!' Cody roared in anguish, then turned and saw Pye standing there with the gun still in his hand. The sheriff had a look of triumph on his double-chinned face. Donald, standing beside him, looked as if he would rather be anywhere else but here today, at this moment. Cody felt a storm of anger shake through him.

'Got the bastard,' said Pye.

Cody gave a loud roar, pointed his gun upwards and fired one, two, three, four, five times, until the chamber was empty then turned and threw the weapon over the side.

'Time to finish off the rest,' said Pye. 'You all right, kid? I just did what you would've done anyway.'

The two men came forward while Cody looked for and fetched his own weapons from where they were lying far apart on the scrub-laden ground. He did not trust himself to speak, knowing only that he would be roaring imprecations at Pye.

Pye came forward, peering cautiously over the edge, but as he started to do so, there was another roar and the whole area on which they stood seemed to shake as if struck by a minor earthquake. Pye staggered and would have fallen over the edge had it not been for Donald, who was standing near and who put out a strong right arm to hold him. Cody did nothing as he stood there with his reacquired guns, staring darkly at the lawman.

When the noise subsided they heard wild whoops and yells from down below, then the sound of horses' hoofs. The five remaining members of the Mosse gang were free, escaping through a gap they had blown in the wooded pass that gave access to where the gold was hidden. They were free to get out and were doing so as quickly as possible.

'They're leaving without their gold,' said Donald. 'That's kind of strange.'

'No it ain't,' snapped Cody. 'These

are hard men who won't let anythin' stand in their way. No point getting the gold if they're under attack. Don't you an' that fat dog understand? They're out to get us all.'

Donald looked at him with wide eyes.

'Jean,' he said, 'Mary.'

Cody took him by the lapels and, even though Donald was a much bigger man, the younger shook him like a terrier worrying a bone.

'They hid, tell me they're still where I left them.'

'No,' said Donald faintly. 'They're at the entrance to the canyon.'

Cody was not a man to waste any time. He ran forward, leaping over the rocks like a mountain goat, sliding down the broken trail ten times faster than he had climbed. The two older men followed at a more sedate pace forced on them by age and build.

Cody did not even look back. He ran along the rocky ledge that had once sheltered Parsons, dangled off it and dropped to where Satan was still standing. The big horse was pawing at the ground as if he sensed what his master wanted him to do.

Cody loosed the reins with a sweep of his hand and urged the big horse forward just as the rest of the Mosse gang rounded the bend that led to the main part of Bear Canyon. None was as fast as Satan, who rode the trail as if his namesake were on his heels. Cody held his body low and encouraged Satan to move on, knowing that every inch he could gain on the gang would help him save the other travellers.

Finally he was at the settlement. It did his heart good to see that none of the others was visible. They had enough sense to hide. He, himself, had enough sense to ride the stallion over to one of the rocky houses, where he jumped up on the roof, ordered the horse to go, which Satan, who looked after number one, did with a great whinny, then Cody lay low, pulling out his guns at the same moment. He had fired quite a few bullets in his confrontation with Kane. He wriggled further on to the roof of the building hoping he would be concealed enough as he reloaded his weapons. He heard the now familiar voice of McCourt shouting to his men.

'Ride round, boys, keep those weapons drawn. I'll go back down an' shoot the other riders.' Cody knew that he meant Pye and Donald.

Cody pushed himself to the edge of the roof and saw the other four men milling around.

'There's one,' shouted a big brute of a man. At first Cody thought he had been spotted then he saw the man aim at the entrance to the pass. Then Clemens ran out. He carried the shotgun he had been handed by Donald when the latter had gone to look for Cody.

'Eat this,' he said to the brute, pointed and fired. There was an almighty roar magnified by the stone walls of the canyon. The top of the man's head vanished and his brains and blood sprayed out behind him. The man continued to sit for a short while, and then his nerveless fingers let go of the reins and his body crashed to the ground.

There was a hail of gunfire in the direction of Clemens from the rest of the men. Half-a-dozen holes appeared on his body and a bright flower of red sprang up on his neck, flinging him backwards on to the soil. His body twitched convulsively for a second even though life had already departed.

The three remaining members of the Mosse gang quickly became two when Cody took aim and shot one of the outlaws through the head. The bullet took the man sideways, toppling him off his horse so quickly that when his opened head splattered on the ground it made a huge, red stain.

The other two turned and began shooting at the man on the roof, pinning him down with their fire. If he had even raised his head he would be killed. Cody pulled his body down low, making the split decision to roll off the side of the building and come out with guns blazing. That decision was nullified when the matting on the roof gave way so that with a splintering groan from the material he fell through into the building. He lay there for a second, stunned by his fall. He was lucky he had not been impaled on a jagged splinter of wood. The wound on his forehead was throbbing again, but this time with a pulse of anger. He picked up his gun from the feet of the corpses in that desolate room, a woman and a man, then made his way to the door. It had gone strangely silent outside. He kicked the door open, running out because a moving target is harder to hit, his guns at the ready, but saw only two riderless horses which trotted away, whinnying loudly. The two men had run for cover.

'Over here,' shouted a gruff voice. He looked over to the entrance of the canyon and saw a sight that froze the blood in his veins.

* * *

In the meantime, McCourt thought he would get easy pickings. It was clear to him that he had two men to deal with, but while the rest were finishing the young upstart he would dispatch these two then get back together with the men, fetch the gold and settle down. It did not seem to occur to him that perhaps the gold was the main source of their problems and that more killings might make them so wanted they would never get the peace to enjoy their ill-gotten treasure.

Donald had been all for getting their horses and joining the fray, but Pye was more cautious. He saw the stranger riding back to where they had hidden in the long grass. He jumped up and his guns spat fire at the newcomer. McCourt was thrown off his mount, but he landed a distance away from them and hid behind some boulders, from where he fired at them. Pye gave a low groan as a bullet seared the side of his fat body. Donald, who thought only of his daughter, got up and ran over to the spot where the man lay, shooting as he went. McCourt knew that he would be killed if he remained where he was, because he was unable to accurately draw a line of fire on the roaring, moving merchant. The outlaw jumped to his feet and faced his attacker.

Donald did not become a sitting duck. He threw his body to one side, firing at the same time. McCourt gave a roar of pain as a bullet took him in the midriff. He clutched at his belly and fell down, still roaring in pain. Donald took aim and shot him in the head.

It was a kindness really.

He went back to the sheriff and helped Pye to his feet. Despite the pain, the lawman would live, as the wound was superficial.

'Now, let's get to the fray,' said Donald. All traces of the peace-loving merchant were now gone. He eyes had a fixed look and his jaw was tight with anger. Together the two men mounted up — Pye with some difficulty — and went to join Cody.

Cody saw that the two men were leading Jean and Mary into the entrance, guns at their heads.

'My name's Gibson,' said the man walking with Mary. 'Now, you just put down your weapons and we'll let them go.'

'Don't do it,' screamed Mary, struggling with the man, 'they'll kill you.'

'Better than that,' said Gibson, 'put down your weapons and we'll all go down and get that there gold. Fetch the horses and lead them now. But first put down your guns.' Cody did as he was told. He flung his guns to one side.

'Thanks,' said Jean, glaring at him as the other outlaw kept a steady aim at her head. 'You've just condemned us all to death.'

Cody was not one to justify his actions. He fetched the two horses and they all began walking down the canyon. It was a long way to the pass, but it meant that the two thieves would retain control over them. Now that Cody was weaponless, though, they made the three of them stand in line while they mounted. Then they rode behind while their new slaves walked forward. It was obvious they, along with McCourt, would use them and shoot them afterwards as they rode off with their loot.

At that moment Donald and the sheriff came around the corner. They saw what was happening and immediately opened fire. Cody grabbed both the women and pulled them into the stony walls of the canyon then ran forward. The two criminals were concentrating on their new enemy. He dodged the flailing hoofs of his horse, and then pulled Gibson by the leg, hauling him off the saddle. Gibson pointed his gun upwards but Cody kicked it out of his hands. Gibson got up to run, but Pye shot him in the back. The man fell forward and clawed briefly at the dusty ground before expiring.

The other rider, knowing that McCourt must be dead and that he was on his own, gave up the fight, grabbed the reins of his horse and turned to flee but a shot to the neck from Pye dispatched him as well.

'Saves hangin' them,' said the sheriff, dismounting stiffly and walking over to inspect the corpses to make sure there was no sign of life. It wouldn't be the first time a 'dead' man had turned over and taken a potshot at him.

In the meantime Cody went over to the two women.

'Are you all right?'

'No thanks to you,' said Jean bitterly. Cody saw that even Mary lowered her gaze when she looked at him.

The young man could have pointed out that he did not want to risk their lives, that once they were down where the gold was he would have found a way to help get them out of the mess they were in even if it had cost him his own life, but he had been misunderstood from the moment he got there.

His face hardened and he walked away from them.

'Let's get your gold,' he said.

13

Less than an hour later the wagon was at the pass. None of the party was really speaking that much to one another. It was Pye who took charge of the operation. He seemed to have come into his own.

When they got down to the pass, what had once been a wide entrance was now a narrow gap surrounded by soil and rocks which had just been wide enough for the gang members to get their horses through, blasted by the dynamite they carried for their illegal operations. Inside the valley the gold was still sitting on the carriage left by the now dead criminals.

'What we'll do,' said Pye, 'is pass the gold through to the other side and load it on to the other wagon, then just plain get out of here.'

'Wait a minute, who's staying on

this side and who's loading on the other?' asked Cody. 'Do you really trust this big skunk?' he asked Jean and Mary.

'I think we'll get you and Donald to pass out the gold,' said Jean. 'Then I can supervise and load from the other side. Mary, you can stay with us.'

'That makes sense,' said Cody. 'I'm still the maverick, eh, even though you've seen what he's like? You don't trust me enough.'

'It's not that,' said Jean. 'You're a lot fitter than Pye. Even if we bring the wagon with the gold closer, we still have to carry the bullion through.'

This mollified Cody somewhat. He was bruised and beaten from the events of the last few hours, but he was indeed probably the fittest and strongest person here next to Mary.

'Besides,' said Jean, 'I've come to a decision about this gold. You see, I've known all along, it isn't ours to have.'

The others looked at her as if she had taken a touch of the sun.

'Come on, Pye, you know what I mean, don't you?' She looked directly at the sheriff.

'All right, guess there's a story attached. Let's just say the territory was finalizing a land deal with the Mexicans an' decided to pay them a couple of million dollars for the deal. Them Mexicans don't want paper dollars, they want gold because bullion not only doesn't lose its value, the value goes up. Does that sound right, Jean?'

'Yes, it does.' Jean decided to continue with the story. 'Kane was a personable young man at the time. He worked for Federal Land Agency, but this was only as a pretext. He was really finding out information for the Mosse gang. Jake was his supervisor.'

'Yep, and together they decided it might be worthwhile liberating that there gold and starting a new life,' said Pye.

'So the gold was sent out, overland, to go to the authorities in Mexico,' said Jean. 'It was guarded by four state troopers and accompanied by Jake and Kane.'

'Little bit of trouble happened,' said Pye. 'The Mosse gang attacked the wagon. They thought it would be a walkover, but they was chased off by the troopers. Trouble was, when the guards came back — less of 'em than before, and with prisoners, the gold was gone and so were Jake and Kane. The gold was never recovered an' eventually wound up here. Don't know what story Jake spun them settlers so he could conceal it here.'

'Then Kane knew where it was all the time?' asked Cody. 'Why did he bother tracking down Jake and taking his map?'

''Cos Kane didn't know. You see, Mosse ratted Kane out just before he was hanged for attacking the consignment. Kane was caught in the desert where he had been knocked out and abandoned by Jake, and sentenced to two years in Yuma — although he denied the charges — just in case he was guilty. The rest of the gang scattered. He kept silent because he didn't want his full involvement to be known, and also because he swore that one day he was coming back for Jake Thatcher.' Pye finished his speech and glared at Jean. 'That's all in the past, now let's get this yellow stuff loaded an' get out of here. I lost Jackson an' Bud because of this. The least I can do is get some kind of reward for all this trouble.'

'A reward is what we'll be getting,' said Jean, 'but not by depositing the money in the bank.'

They all looked at her as if she had gone mad.

'Jake marked his map wrong deliberately,' said Jean calmly. 'He knew that if Kane ever caught up with him, he would die. He wanted to mislead Kane and drive him mad looking for the gold. But Jake was truly sorry for what he had done. He spent so freely because it was guilty money that he had in his possession. He wanted to turn the Slash

T into a good business, one which would see us into our old age, then he wanted to forget the other money even existed. But the ranch wasn't always in profit, and when you know how to get hold of money easily, the temptation is always there. When Kane arrived at our home, I think Jake was just ready to go. He couldn't live with himself. He made Kane kill him.'

'I don't understand what this has to do with this situation,' said Mary.

'It's simple enough, my dear. Pye knows as well as I do, that this gold is part of a loan to the territory by the Federal Reserve. Spending this money is a form of treason. What would you do with the gold, Cody?'

'I don't want it,' said that young man promptly. 'I wish I'd never seen or heard of any of this.'

'You see? A bit idealistic maybe, but Cody has the right idea. This money has to be returned to the authorities.'

'How do we do that?'

'We'll go to Phoenix and let them

know we have it in a safe place, make a sworn deposition of how it was returned.'

'Tell you what,' said Pye reasonably, 'let's go in and see what's left, make a tally before we set out, then we know what we can do for the authorities.'

They went into the valley. Pye made straight for the wagon on to which the gold had been loaded, but Cody looked around the space and finally found the body of his brother. Kane had landed on some scrub and bushes, which meant that his body was more or less intact except for the bullet wounds that had ended his life before he had hit the ground. Cody fetched one of the spades that the men had been using to turn over the rocky soil once it had been blasted, getting it out of the way during their search. Mary saw what he was doing, and without a word she came over and helped him to lift his brother over to one of the holes in the ground dug by the gang. Cody said nothing, but accepted her help gratefully as he put his brother to rest, folding his hands over his chest and closing his eyes. Since there was plenty of rock and soil around due to their blasting operations, it wasn't hard for him to cover the body. Mary finished the job by getting a couple of dry branches, breaking them to size and binding them together in the shape of a cross. Cody put this at the head of his brother's grave.

'We should do the same with the rest,' said Mary, and then walked away. Cody could see that she had still not forgiven him for throwing his guns down earlier.

The others had finished their work. None of them had remarked at all on Cody's actions. Kane had been his brother.

'We can start now,' said Jean, taking charge of the operation. 'Once we get out of here we'll send a scout in to the capital and state what we know, an armed escort will come out and take the bullion back, then we'll confirm what happened and claim the reward. Once they realize we're telling the truth the money'll be forthcoming. We just won't lean too heavily on the amount Jake managed to spend.'

'Good idea,' said Pye, then he began strolling thoughtfully away from the group, all of whom were standing beside the carriage on which rested the gold. This included Cody, who had come over after dealing with his brother's final resting place.

'As for the reward money, Cody, Mary and Donald can have it as far as I'm concerned. If I need to sell the ranch I will. What happened here doesn't rest easily with me.'

'Rests a bit better with me,' said Pye. They all looked over to where he stood with his back to the rocky entrance to the valley. He held both his newly loaded guns up in a manner that showed he would brook no interference with his plans. 'I guess I thought you would be handy to load the bullion for me, because what you're looking at is my retirement fund.' He spat on the ground. 'But I guess this is too good an opportunity to miss when you're all unarmed. It'll be a bit of bother gettin' the gold out, but there's time to rest an' what's a few more dead bodies on top of what's been happenin' here?'

Tired of talking he raised his weapons to finally destroy those who stood in his way.

14

Now that the sheriff had the drop on them he seemed to be quite comfortable with the idea of ending their lives.

'Gonna be a bit of a trial gettin' this back,' he said, referring to the gold, 'but reckon it'll be worth it. I'll be in Texas under a new name in no time, an' live real quiet, just buy a big house and a get a new wife.' He looked regretfully at Jean. 'If you'd been a bit more co-operative we could be doin' this together.'

Jean only glared at him, a man she had once thought of as a friend. But it was evident that she was not going to answer him.

'Look,' said Cody quietly, 'it doesn't need to be like this. Take the gold, but spare their lives. They've done nothing to you, except put some trust into you.' As he spoke, he moved, slowly, almost imperceptibly narrowing the gap between himself and the man who had once represented the law. Pye narrowed his eyes and glared at the young rancher.

'Wouldn't move no more,' he said, 'you'll be the first to get a bullet atween them eyes of yours.'

Cody decided he was going to make the move anyway. If he was going to die he would rather die defending what he loved best and he suddenly realized that Mary, who was standing behind him, was the one he wanted to protect. If he could knock the gun out of Pye's hand maybe there would be a chance for the others to intervene. He resigned himself to his fate; after all, it was better than being hanged. He tensed his muscles to leap forward just as the crooked sheriff tightened his finger on the trigger.

Then the totally unexpected occurred, which is always the way in life — and death. Jean ran forward between the rest of the party and the sheriff. She was so quick in her movements that she caught him by surprise. She grabbed

Pye's forearms and wrestled with him, pulling him back and forth, but he was a large man and she could not knock him off his feet. Pye fought back and managed to free one of his arms, and then he did the unthinkable and shot the widow at point-blank range. Jean spun around as if she had been punched in the face; such was the force with which she had been hit, crumpling to the ground between the two men. She lay and groaned at their feet, a red stain blossoming on her chest.

When Cody saw what was happening he immediately ran forward to help her, but she had been shot within a bare second of tackling the crooked lawman. Cody immediately chopped down on Pye's wrist, making him drop one gun, and then kicked out with a dusty boot at the other gun, which sent it spinning into the air only to land quite a distance from them both.

Pye gave a roar of pain and anger. Instead of trying to retrieve his weapon because he knew that Cody would be on his back, he turned and ran through the rocky entrance to the pass. Cody immediately realized what he was doing. If he could get to the fallen bodies of the gang members a short distance away he would get all the weapons he wanted. Cody picked up the six-gun dropped by the sheriff and ran after him. The sheriff ran with a speed that belied his bulk, weaving as he ran to put the other off his target. But Cody was a wiser man than to attempt to shoot the running man whilst running too. He stood stock still once he was a little closer, took aim, and fired.

The first shot missed. Pye was able to get to the bodies, dived down and grabbed one of the weapons, spun round and fired at Cody, but he shot wild in his haste to kill the young man. Cody heard rather than saw the bullet spit up dust in the ground beside him. He calmly took aim and fired again. The sheriff had already been wounded on the side, now he gave a groan as the bullet entered his leg. At that distance it was not powerful enough to take the leg off, but he fell to one side yelling in pain. Cody swiftly finished the encounter by running forward and knocking the recumbent man out with one blow to the head. He used some leather traces to bind his arms, and then left him where he was and went back to his friends.

Jean was still lying where she had fallen, being attended to by Mary, who had used some of her own petticoats as a makeshift bandage. It was obvious that the older woman was not going to make it. Paradoxically her eyes sparkled as Cody bent down beside her.

'Did you get him?' she asked.

'Yes,' said Cody simply. He cradled her in his arms. This was the woman who had almost got him hanged, yet had given him a means of taking revenge.

'I didn't deserve the gold,' said Jean. 'It was the Devil's coin. We all paid for it.' She coughed, thin pink foam on her lips.

'Rest, Jean,' whispered Mary.

'No. Cody, look after these people. That girl loves you. Promise you'll take the gold back.'

'I will,' he said simply. Her eyes searched his for a moment then she gave a small nod of satisfaction. She coughed again then her eyes dulled over and her head fell to one side. Cody gently allowed her to leave his arms and lie where she was. He looked at the others. He was a man now who could take the leadership forced on to him.

'Let's get on with it, we've got a lot of work to do.'

* * *

Less than a week later a large amount of gold was returned to the authorities. After a great deal of scrutiny their story was accepted and they were told that they would receive a just reward.

Pye, who had been kept alive but tied up during the long ride back, was handed over too. His trial had been swift. He was to get the public hanging he had once promised Cody.

The three of them — Donald, Mary and Cody — took the train as far as Tucson. They would spend a little time there before riding back to Coker Town. Donald had already telegraphed his wife to say that her husband and daughter were not only safe, but in good hands.

Donald and Mary, refreshed and clothed in bright, new garments bought in the city, sat across from Cody, who also wore new clothes. Except for the minor scratches on his face, and the forehead wound that had nearly healed, he looked every inch the young gentleman. He had vowed to take over the Slash T and make it a profitable business. His mother would come from the old homestead to live there, but she would never know what had happened to her older son in Bear Canyon; that would be too painful. She would only know that he had passed away on a raid so she could mourn him. Now he looked at Mary. It was not in his nature to go down on one knee.

Donald, who knew the signs, smiled benevolently.

'You have all my blessing, young man,' he said.

'Mary.' Cody smiled and took her hand. 'Will you marry me?'

'Yes,' she said, 'but I did nothing to help you in that place.'

'You saved my life way back when, so I'm going to give you my life,' he told her.

The train thundered on, taking them home.

We do hope that you have enjoyed reading this large print book.

Did you know that all of our titles are available for purchase?

We publish a wide range of high quality large print books including:
Romances, Mysteries, Classics
General Fiction
Non Fiction and Westerns

Special interest titles available in large print are:
The Little Oxford Dictionary
Music Book, Song Book
Hymn Book, Service Book

Also available from us courtesy of Oxford University Press:
Young Readers' Dictionary
(large print edition)
Young Readers' Thesaurus
(large print edition)

For further information or a free brochure, please contact us at:
Ulverscroft Large Print Books Ltd.,
The Green, Bradgate Road, Anstey,
Leicester, LE7 7FU, England.
Tel: (00 44) **0116 236 4325**
Fax: (00 44) **0116 234 0205**

Jason Brand's latest assignment takes him into the mountains, searching for two missing men — a Deputy US Marshal and a government geologist. But this apparently routine assignment turns out to be anything but. For Bodie the Stalker, hunting a brutal killer, rides the same trail. It's just another manhunt for him — until he finds himself on the wrong end of the chase. But then Bodie meets Brand. And when they join forces, it's as if Hell itself has come to the high country . . .

GUNS OF THE BRASADA

Neil Hunter

Ballard and McCall are in Texas, working for Henry Conway, an old friend, on the Lazy-C ranch. But trouble is brewing: Yancey Merrick, owner of the big Diamond-M, kept pushing to expand his empire. Then Henry's son Harry is run down through the brasada thicket before being shot in the back and killed. Determined to find the guilty party, Ballard and McCall suddenly find themselves deep in a developing range war . . .

LONELY RIDER

Steve Hayes

He calls himself 'Melody', after the
word burned inside his belt. Because
he can't remember his own name
— or anything at all prior to the past
six weeks. It's 'amnesia', according
to Regan Avery, the woman he
rescues from a fast-flowing river. But
Melody doesn't need the fancy
name for his predicament to know
he's in trouble — for the few things
he *can* remember involve being shot
at and wounded, with a posse hard
on his heels . . .